ENTICED BY A HOOD LEGEND

MICHAY

Enticed by A Hood Legend
Copyright 2019 by Michay

Published by Mz. Lady P Presents

All rights reserved

ACKNOWLEDGMENTS

First and foremost, I want to give thanks to God for giving me the strength and courage to write these amazing books. Without him, none of this would be possible. Shout out to my wonderful publisher who saw the potential in me and gave me a chance. All the wisdom she instilled in me remained, and I did exactly what she told me and never folded. Thank you, Mz. Lady P for everything.

To my kids Shaniyah and Jamell, I thank you for putting up with my absence during the times when I was always busy. Just remember mommy has plans for both of you and will always hold you to the highest honor.

Thanks to my wonderful mother and father who helped me during times like this. You guys rock.

Finally, to all my pen sisters under Mz. Lady P Presents, you guys are amazing. We all work very hard to drop these books under nothing but pressure. When I felt like giving up due to my illness, y'all weren't having that. Together we write, and together we conquer. Thanks a million for the encouragement daily.

To my readers who have been rocking with me from day one, I

couldn't do what I do if it weren't for you guys. The feedback and constant support is what keep me going as well. As long as you guys continue to support, I will continue to drop nonstop. Keep dreaming, and those dreams will turn into reality. Love you guys tremendously.

MORE FROM MICHAY

WAYS TO CONNECT WITH MICHAY

Email: mvaughn1991@gmail.com
IG: authoress_michay
Twitter: Authoress Michay
Facebook: Micha Michay

ONE
LEGEND JACKSON

"Welcome home, bro!" my sister Nastasia yelled as soon as I came into the house.

Just seeing my people that never left my side made me feel good — my homies Duce, Nytrell, Nyquan, and Troy. These were my main niggas since high school. They looked out for a nigga hard.

"Thanks, y'all."

"Pop those bottles so we can get lit," my right hand man Duce said.

Everyone began to pop bottle after bottle, and I was all for it. My mom and uncle, who held my crib down while I was away, made sure that my bills were paid on time every month. I can't thank them enough. My uncle was the DJ, and my sister had cooked up a soul food meal with her husband that was right up my alley.

Being gone for seven years, I missed out on a lot, including seeing my nephew being born. I promised myself I would never go back. This was the best feeling in the world to be home.

"I'm glad you home, bro. Shit has been crazy," Nyquan said while handing me a drink.

He was still selling drugs and constantly getting locked up, the same shit since I left. When I left, I passed everything to him hoping that he would flip it and leave the game. I realized I made a big mistake.

"I'm not going back. I just know to keep those square ass niggas out my circle. Niggas were never built for this life."

I got locked up when the police came and raided my trap house. I tried to fight the case, but we found out it was a rat in our circle. Steve was the rat. He was a police informant. They paid him a million dollars, and he went ghost after that. It took everything in me not to have someone off his ass. After having that man-to-man talk with my uncle, I had to let the situation go.

"I know how you feel. Now that you're out, let's get back on track. I'm tryna stack more bread. I'm tryna get the money we used to get before all of this happened."

"That shit is dead. I got enough money in the bank to start up a business, so I'm done with that shit."

He had the nerve to try to get me to get back in the game knowing that I just did seven long years. He's trippin' hard. I was sentenced to ten years, but I got out after doing seven. If I fuck up, I gotta go back to finish the remaining time.

"Now let's party," my mom, who was the nosiest lady I know, said and everyone was starting to get lit. She must have overheard us.

"I want to thank God for sending my baby home to his family. Let whatever happened in the past be a wakeup call. These pigs don't give a fuck about a young brother like you. It's time to build for your future."

We all toast to me coming home. One thing about my mom was that she didn't hold back. She was a strong woman. After our father died, months before Nastasia was born, she has been our father. Nastasia never met him, and I don't have a clear vision of who he was.

"Niggas get out of jail and forget to wash their ass. Why the fuck you still got yo jail suit on?"

I laughed so damn hard at Nytrell that I began choking on my drink. I was fucked up in the head when they told me that he was smoking crack. Life hit him real hard. I never wanted any of my people to hit rock bottom, so I'm definitely gonna get him back on the right track.

"Fuck you, bitch." He then flamed up a blunt. I didn't smoke behind him because ain't no telling where he been putting his lips.

"Yo, Legend, look who just walked in?"

I looked up, and my eyes were playin' tricks on a nigga. It was my crush Onari, her grandma Rosie, and her daughter Aniyah. Onari was Nytrell and Nyquan little sister.

"Onari. That was supposed to be my wife ten years ago."

I have been in love with Onari ever since my sister Nastasia brought her around. The moment I laid eyes on her, I knew she was a good girl. She was a redbone, who stood about five foot four and weighed about one hundred ninety pounds with her long, black curly hair and light brown eyes. She had a body out of this world. I'm not big on body images because those be the birdbrain bitches with no sense of direction. I liked her because she didn't need to show her cheeks or thighs to get attention. She was also shy, quiet, and had her own daycare. However, I do know if you fuck with her, she turns into a monster. She always stood out because everything she did was different.

"You better go get ya girl," Duce said, but I was already on it. She has turned me down about ten times, so maybe eleven will be my lucky number.

I finished my drink and walked over to her while she was talking to my sister.

"Long time no see, Onari. How you doing, Ms. Rosie?" I flashed my all white teeth, and Onari giggled.

"Hey, son, they done finally let you out, huh?" She hugged me and kissed my cheeks.

When we were young niggas running through the hood, Ms. Rosie always hid us from the police. Afterwards, she would curse us out, and we were every stupid mother fucker in the book.

"Thanks, Legend. I see you haven't changed." She knew I didn't give a fuck about her having a man.

"Nope, not at all."

"Well, it was good seeing you. I have to get home so that I can get my classroom ready for tomorrow."

She began to get her daughter's coat on, and I was starting to get baby fever. When my ex-girlfriend lost our baby boy at birth three months before I got locked, that shit tore me up. It was so painful that she walked away. I never thought I would get baby fever, but Aniyah was giving me just that.

"Nice seeing you again. I'ma see you later." I reached down and hugged her. I also walked her and her grandma to the car and made sure they drove away safely.

A COUPLE OF DAYS LATER, I was inside my office tryna figure out my next move. I had both of my lawyers, uncle, and my homie Duce, Nytrell, and Nyquan. These were the only people that I let into my world, and that know everything about me.

"So, what are your plans? Whatever it is, it has to be legit," one of my lawyers said. He was tired of me having run-ins with the law. Although I pay him a hefty penny, he still cares for us all.

"I plan on getting my construction license back so that when my plans do fall through, things will be legit. I'ma play it smart. The good thing is all I have to do is go to school to get one hundred and fifty hours and then I'm good. I just have to get permission from city hall first. Hopefully, my background won't be a problem."

"Don't worry about that right now. You know I got you on that end." I nodded, and nothing else needed to be said. They knew there is no stopping me when I made my mind up.

"Well, you got most of it planned out, but since your still under the police raider for other crimes they say you committed, you have to move smart. That means let the niggas go that are in the way and not helping you to the top. Even though the judge reduced your sentence, that doesn't mean they won't come after you again. Stay woke, nephew."

My uncle was everything. He had all my money put away for when I got home. He didn't touch a dime, which is why I will forever hold him down.

"I hear you. I'ma keep my head up." We talked a little bit more before they left me to myself.

I never understood when my mom said when you get older, you get wiser until now. I'ma be thirty-one February fifteenth, and I plan on making the best of it. I missed out on precious years that I can't get back. I stayed up all night writing things on what I want my vision to be. If I don't go hard for myself, no one else will. Once the clock struck eight the next morning, I jumped in the shower and was out for the count. I wasn't sleeping that long before I got woke up to some bad news.

Nastasia called me crying saying that our uncle was killed hours after they left my house. I was beyond fucked up in the head. I just wanted to come home to some peace. It's crazy because as soon as I get out, bullshit starts. My uncle practically raised us with my mom since he was the only male figure in our lives. At one point, I was calling him dad, but when I got older, I knew he was just my uncle.

I immediately put some clothes on and drove to my sister's crib. Seeing all the police and red tape made this shit real. I parked on the street and got out my car.

Walking up to the house, most of our family members were already there, including her friend Onari, Troy, and her brothers. Everyone came and hugged me, including Onari. I was gone be ok, but my mom wasn't. It's like she felt safe with him since I went to jail. The police had everything taped off so we couldn't enter the house.

"Aye, just say the word, and it's whatever." Duce was ready to shut some shit down. He was loud and making a scene.

"Naw, I got a feeling this wasn't no nigga in the streets."

"How you figure that?"

"If a nigga wanted my uncle, why wait until I get out. The shit doesn't add up. Most of those cops out there wanted my head, and since my uncle wouldn't give them information on me, they took matters into their own hands. He wasn't into these streets."

I was low-key hurting behind this shit. I honestly believed the police was behind this shit — they're known for paying snitches. They're also known for killing some of these niggas in the streets.

"It's all good. Remember we have to play this shit smart. Keep your head into building your brand and watch how shit starts coming out. If these cops had anything to do with this shit, they gone get dealt with," Troy said, and once again, I knew I had to keep it cool.

"No doubt."

I stayed there with my family once the police left to make sure everyone was ok. Duce, Troy, and I cleaned up all the blood while everyone else went down in the basement. I didn't want them seeing that shit. I didn't even wanna go back home, so most of us stayed there until the next morning. We needed answers, and we were definitely gone get them.

TWO

ONARI WILLIAMS

It felt good being back in my classroom after this winter break. I was missing my little babies, and at the same time, I was glad to be away from my boyfriend, Pike. It seemed like things drastically changed when I started making more money than him. He even refused to watch our daughter Aniyah, so my grandma would help me out.

It went from us working together to Pike complaining about splitting the bills. My grandma helps me with the bills since she stays with me. We live in a five-bedroom house near Lake Shore Drive that we're still paying for after my granddad died. She wanted to give it up, but I couldn't let her do that. This house was in the family, and I wanted it to stay that way. We didn't know he was in debt, so we had to pick up his mess. I loved this place because the view is amazing at night, and I can do my early morning runs and feel safe, or so I thought.

Now, Pike has turned into this insecure ass man. He quit his job all of a sudden just to sit in the house and watch TV all damn day. To make matters worse, I found out he was smoking crack with my brother Nytrell, so I put him out. He begged me to help him get clean, and because he was the father of my daughter, I did. I paid for him to go to rehab hoping that everything would go back to normal. Pike was clean for a month, and things went back downhill, so I gave up. Something I won't do is take care of a grown ass man.

It was always just me, my mom, dad, and two brothers, Nytrell and Nyquan growing up in my household. My dad used to show my brothers and me the difference between real men and street thugs. He taught them how to love and cherish your lady friends. I was told no man in the streets could do anything for me.

When my dad introduced me to Pike at a church function, I just knew he was the one. Every time we went out, he wore his best suit and shoes and always kept his hair cut completely bald. I was never big on looks. I just wanted someone who I could have fun with and carry this relationship for years.

When my parents got killed in a car crash, Pike got bold and said fuck us. Even though I was twenty-one at the time, I needed him the most. I had to lean on my grandma for support. To this day, I have to thank my grandmother for stepping up. She was dealing with the death of her husband as well as both my parents. It was hard, but we made it.

For my brothers, growing up was hard because they always got teased because of their eyes. They both were born blind in one eye, so they have a gray eye and light brown eye. I got lucky, I guess. Nytrell being the oldest at twenty-nine, went down the wrong path when he started smoking crack. Before all of this, he was the nigga in the street. He and Nyquan were always getting mistaken for twins. We each were a year apart, where I was twenty-seven and Nyquan was twenty-eight. My brothers both had dreadlocks with a caramel skin tone. They stood about six foot one and weighed about two hundred pounds even. Bitches loved their weight, especially Nyquan, who had a lot of money from selling drugs. He also had three boys that he took care of faithfully.

Now, Nytrell looks like he's homeless because of the drugs. He now weighs about one hundred twenty pounds. One thing my grandma told me was to never give up on him. That's something I could never do. My brothers are my everything, and I will hold them down through whatever, even though the decisions they make I don't agree with.

"Hey, boo. Sorry, I'm a little late."

Nastasia, who's been my best friend since grammar school, was one of my assistance. She's been off for two days because her uncle was killed. That shit was still unbelievable. My daycare was small. I only take babies from one year to three years old, the max being fifteen kids. I also offer after school for the older kids for two hours max for the moms that need extra help.

"How are you holding up?"

"I'ma be ok. I'm just glad to be in a different environment because it's too sad around my house. My mom doesn't want to leave his house, and I don't want to be there. I keep seeing all that blood." She looked like she hadn't slept in days.

"Good. We got a lot of paperwork to fill out for the new year. We have to update parents on a lot of things, especially sending them with no warm clothes."

I handed her a stack of papers and started getting breakfast ready for when they come in. I knew putting her right to work would get her mind off that situation.

IT TOOK me almost thirty minutes to prepare breakfast, and when I finished, Pike was sitting in my office as if I invited him.

"One of my homies called and told me you had a nigga in here. Fuck is up with you? I'm not about to play these games with yo young dumb ass."

He really tried to chew my ass up with no evidence. I also noticed his mouth was white in the corner, which let me know he had just finished getting high. I just laughed because he was the definition of a clown.

"Boy, fuck you. You in yo feelings for shit. I also told you I'm not dealing with you getting high. You worried about the wrong shit."

"Oh, I'm a boy now? Ain't nobody smoking shit?"

"Yes, Pike. Your thirty-five acting like you're twenty. I'm not about to do this with you anymore. I'm twenty-seven tryna build my brand, and you're not helping me build. You're trying your best to bring me down to your level, and I won't allow it."

He stood up like he was gone hit me, and I was ready. One thing Pike never did was raise his hands at me. My dad and brothers taught me how to throw these hands whenever I need to. Weak bitch doesn't run in my blood.

"So, because I lost my job, you're just basically saying fuck me?"

"You quit your job. It's a big difference. I can't take care of you, pays all these bills, and two car notes. You also smoking crack, and I don't want no man like that. If I'ma struggle, let me struggle on my own."

I was fed up with him. He acted like I owed him something. He didn't even want to give me kids after so many years, let alone marry me. Aniyah was not planned, and for a long time, he was pissed.

"Aight bet. Say no more. I'ma be back to get my things." He tossed my house keys on the table and tried to leave.

"Ah-ah, drop the car keys as well." He threw them at me and walked out.

"Nastasia, lock that door until eight a.m. I don't want him walking back in here."

"Girl, I'm glad he's gone. What the fuck is his problem?"

"I don't know, but he got me fucked up. We barely communicate, let alone have sex. All he wants is for me to leave him money to get a drink and fix his food. I don't feel like a girlfriend."

"Duuuhh. You were never his girlfriend. I told you before there were rumors that he got someone else pregnant and she's way older than you. Oh, let's not forget she still stays at home with her mom." I wasn't surprised by the news because I heard it before. I'm just not that bitch that's about to fight over some unemployed dick. I will not.

"Girl, fuck him and her. My money won't stop, and neither will my sleep." She smiled like she had something up her sleeve.

"Bitch, why you laughing?" I smirked, and she walked back to her office. Once my kids started coming in, one of my lunch ladies told me that I had company.

"Is it Pike?"

"No, it's a handsome light skinned dude. He is sexy, girl. He's got tattoos covering his neck and arms. He's gotten comfortable out there chilling on the couch."

The only dude I know that's light skinned with lots of tattoos is Legend. I was hesitant, and it didn't make things better because he sent me a text.

Legend: *Man, stop playing those crackhead games and bring yo ass out here.*

I'ma kill Nastasia for giving him my number. While my helper was in the room, I tiptoed into the lounge area.

Legend has always been that nigga. At first, I thought that was a street name, but it turned out it was his real name. When I first met him, he would stalk me morning, noon, and night. He would beg my brothers to get me to go out with him, but I couldn't. I also knew he was in the streets heavy, and I wasn't that chick. Bitches were lined up just to get a piece of him, but his attention was always on me. I turned him down every time.

I was peeking around the corner so that he couldn't see me. He has always been a chill type of nigga. He always kept his hair curled or cut, and made sure he kept his cars and cribs on point. Legend was about five foot eight and had a body out this world. He used to always get me wearing those damn gray jogging pants, with his dick slinging north, south, east, and west. I knew bitches were begging for the dick.

"Bitch, my brother is single and he doesn't fuck around in the streets anymore." Nastasia practically pushed me into the lounge, and he looked up.

"Damn, I thought I was gone have to kidnap you."

"Whatever? How are you feeling?" I was referring to his uncle being killed. Nastasia was taking it hard even though she tried to downplay it, so I made sure to check on her every hour.

"It's life, man. Shit happens. Enough about me, what time you get off?" he boldly asked me with a straight face.

"Four or five."

"Ok, be ready around eight. I'ma take you out to eat."

I couldn't even protest because he got up, kissed me on my cheeks, and walked out. I was blushing so hard that I couldn't even focus. It's like I see a whole new person in him. Years ago, I probably would have cursed him out for coming to my job.

"Ok, back to reality." Nastasia came behind me, and I laughed.

Once I got him off my mind, I focused on my babies.

WHEN OUR DAY ENDED, I ran home to get myself together. I haven't been on a date in so long that I couldn't control myself. I wasn't looking for a relationship at the moment, but I don't mind the company either.

Since it was cold outside, I threw on some black fitted jeans and a fitted black shirt with some gray wedges to top it off. I pinned my natural hair up in a bun and let my edges fall. I gave myself a double look in the mirror before applying my red lipstick.

I was about to pour me some wine, but the doorbell rung, and I knew it was Legend. He was real bold and always have been. I guess Nastasia gave him my address as well. I'm not mad though because she offered to watch Aniyah since my grandma wasn't feeling good.

My grandma had diabetes, and when her legs swell, she can barely walk. The first thing he asked when Legend walked in was where my grandma. He went to make sure she was ok and if she needed anything. He has always been crazy about her and vice versa.

"You look gorgeous." He kissed my cheeks then handed me some flowers— shit I never received before.

"Thanks. You look nice as well."

He was rocking a simple Kenzo outfit and some black Timber-lands. Knowing Legend all these years, he will put some shit together and have everyone complimenting him.

"Let's roll." He grabbed my hand, took my house keys, and locked the door. Once again, I was speechless.

THREE

NYTRELL WILLIAMS

Sitting in my buddy's car getting high was the best feeling in the world. It's like the feeling gets better every time. I couldn't stop and didn't plan on it either. This was my life ever since my parents were killed in a car crash. It started right after I graduated high school.

I started smoking squares because I was always paranoid, and then it turned to drinking. That didn't help the way I felt, so I then went to smoking leaf. That shit had me doing off the wall shit like stealing from my sister and grandma. My last option was crack, and I never let up on it. The way it made me feel was the best feeling in the world because all my pain went away. Every time my family tried to get me clean, I turn them down. This is my life, and it is what it is.

"You cool, bitch?" my homie Rondo said while giggling like a lil bitch. I hated the way he laughed. He sounded like a female.

"G, I told you about that faggot shit. I'm not with that shit. Get yo laugh together." He ignored me and then suddenly blurted out we need to rob someone for some cash.

"I'm not fucking with it because shit went all bad with Legend's uncle." The plan was for us to go into his crib and get the safe I knew he had, but it wasn't there. Things went bad when he came from out of nowhere, and tried to shoot us, but Rondo was too fast. He shot him to death, and we got out of there.

"Man, Legend ain't gone find out. You did tell me he was thinking the police did it, right?"

"Yea, but I'm not fucking with it. Legend with have our heads if he finds out what we did." He was persistent.

"Ok, what about yo sister? I know she's got some cash lying around."

"Naw, all her money be in the bank. The only way we could get access to her money without her knowing is if we recruit Pike. He'll be all for it since he moved out. We just have to make sure they're not there."

"So, if we make plans now, we could figure out how we gone do this." I agreed with him and finished getting high.

AN HOUR LATER, I woke up, and Rondo was gone. I guess he went back out to get his fix. I, on the other hand, was sick to my stomach and needed some food. I went straight to my sister and granny's crib, which I slept here from time to time. The moment I opened the door, my grandma greeted me with a warm smile.

"Hey, grandma. How you feeling? I see your legs are back swollen." She was limping but could never sit down.

"Yea, you know they act up when it's about to snow. You hungry? I made chili." She didn't even have to ask me that.

"Yes, ma'am."

"Get yo coat off and go wash ya hands," she told me then began to fix my food with a tall glass of Kool-Aid.

She sat at the table with me, while I devoured that chili. She was reading the newspaper about Donald Trump and his bullshit he pulling.

"So, when do you plan on getting yourself together? Life is passing you by." I hated these conversations.

"I don't know. I don't want you to worry about me. I just want you to focus on getting better." I don't know what I'ma do if she leaves this world. At eighty-five, she still had plenty of years on this earth in my eyes.

"I'ma keep praying that God works on you and gets you back healthy. You know I don't judge you, but I do get scared." She began to cry, and I felt bad as hell.

"Grandma, I'ma be ok. You hear me."

I hated when she cries because her blood pressure gets sky high. I got up to hug her. When she calmed down, she went upstairs to get me some towels to wash up and some clean clothes to wear that I had left here. I guess she was letting me know that I stank.

Once I finished eating and taking a shower, I decided to watch *The Chi* with her to keep her calm.

"Where are Onari and Aniyah?" I realized it was quiet. I normally would hear the "Baby Shark" song, and Aniyah screaming like crazy.

"Oh, she went out with my son-in-law Legend, and Nastasia is watching Aniyah. It's peaceful."

"I know."

We talked a little bit more about Legend and how he was a good guy. I agreed with her because Legend was known for helping everyone out. If someone needed their rent paid, he went above and beyond to help them. He also helped people with car notes and other bills. That's why I felt bad as fuck what happened to his uncle. I pray he never finds out.

Just when I noticed my grandma dosing off, I decided to check around the house for some cash. Since the government had shut down, I couldn't get my Link at the moment. That was my way of getting high by selling it. I roamed the house and only found twenty dollars. I went back down and acted as if I never got up. I sat and watched TV until I got a text from Rondo that he came up. That was my cue to leave.

"Granny, I'm heading out now." I woke her up, she told me to be careful, and she locked the door. Rondo was parked out front, and I climbed inside. I immediately got high.

Legend: *Wassup, bro. If you need anything, let me know. You know I got you. Love ya, kid.*

I got a text to my government phone from Legend. Shit like that is why he would always be known as a Legend. His name rang bells throughout Chicago and many other cities.

Me: *Thanks, bro. I really appreciate you. Love you too, bro.*

FOR THE REST of the night, Rondo and I got high, and we eventually called Pike to join us.

"Ok, we got to plan this shit out the right way. We can't fuck up like we did the last time. Shit went crazy." Rondo had this shit planned out.

"Now that Legend is all into Onari's space, we gone have to make sure everyone in the house is gone. We're also gone have to be careful with him popping up. I'm tryna take whatever is valuable, including that big ass flat screen. We tryna get bands off everything we take."

"What about Legend? We have to get him far away as possible. Say someone died or something. I don't trust him being near, and he finds out." I had to know this would go as planned without someone getting hurt.

"Why the fuck nobody told me he was fucking my bitch?" Pike blurted out, and I damn near broke his jaw.

"Watch yo fucking mouth." I said pissed. He was just being insecure because he was out fucking bitches.

"My bad."

"Nigga he just got out. How the fuck he fucking her already. You trippin." Rondo said and I just shook my head.

Rumors are going around that he had a baby on the way by some old ass lady.

"It's not our place to say anything. Just like it wasn't our place to tell Onari you have a kid on the way." Rondo shut him up, and we continued with the plans.

I just hope that shit goes right.

FOUR

LEGEND

"Yo ass don't look like you just got out. You got right out and copped a brand-new Benz," one of the local dudes who was previously working for me said.

I knew he was tryna get some cash, but that shit was dead. Then on top of that, he didn't know what the fuck he was talking about. I'd had this Benz for years now. The only thing I did was upgrade all the parts and added new rims. I just let niggas talk.

"What you on? You tryna get this drink with me?"

I had to laugh to keep from slapping his ass. Here it is. I just got released, and my uncle was killed. I'm not in the mood to play games.

"I'm on getting this money, something you should be doing."

I opened my car door, got in, and drove off. I rode by Onari's crib and rung her bell without a care in the world. I wasn't gone give up this time. I'm out and on bigger and better things.

Pike was gone have to fall back. My sister told me he was a scumbag and always using her for her crib and money. He couldn't even help her with the baby, shit that I hate. Once she opened the door, I handed her some flowers and pulled her to the car.

"Where we going?" She smelled good as fuck in her Rihanna perfume.

"Just sit back and let me do this," I smirked then played that new NBA YoungBoy. His shit was smacking hard.

One thing about me, I never eat at a restaurant more than once, so we took a long ass drive out to Country Club Hill to her favorite restaurant.

"OMG! You remember my favorite place to eat." She was blushing when I pulled up to Olive Garden.

I knew she was big on pasta and salad tryna keep her figure in great shape. I laughed, and we both walked inside. I had already made reservations because this place is always packed. I picked a table in the corner where we could laugh and joke around like old times.

"Follow me in the back, sir." Some nice old lady walked us to our seats.

They had it set up real nice with candles, roses on the table, and a bottle of champagne, everything I asked for. I pulled out her seat for her, and it's like she was in disbelief.

"You ok?" I laughed while sitting down to pour her favorite wine. I knew she wasn't big on drinking, but wine and weed always had her right.

"Yea, I'm just impressed. I mean I know what type of guy you are. I just never received this much treatment."

I took a sip of my water and sat back tryna figure this shit out. This girl was everything in my eyes, and I don't fuck with too many chicks. She had everything most men my age look for in a woman.

"So, you're telling me Pike never took you anywhere?"

"In the beginning, when my dad introduced us, he did. I knew he wanted my father to like him. When my parents died, things changed. He started getting lazy then suddenly fired and expected me to take care of him, not to mention the drug problem."

Before I could respond, the waiter came and took our orders. I ordered her the Cajun pasta, and I ordered a kind of pasta that had steak pieces inside it.

"What's wrong with you helping him out? I mean if y'all been in this shit for years and a nigga falls off, you gotta lift him back up."

I guess she found it funny.

"See, there's a big difference between being a real man, and tryna be a man for show and tell. Pike would invite company over and brag and the little shit he bought. Who does that? Then he all of a sudden wanted me to cook for him and his people like I was a slave. I can count on one hand how many times he cooked tacos. As his woman, I did everything to get him back on track." I just shook my head. That was definitely some coward shit.

"So, what's the status?"

When they brought our food, I started smashing everything.

"Ain't no status. I realized he was never on my level. He gave me my keys back and left. I won't lose no sleep. I just have to give him his things, and we're done."

"So, where do you and I stand? You already know how I feel about you. I'm not the same guy as before. I'm tryna settle down and build a family." I'd been tryna get with this girl since before I was fucking.

"Legend, you know how I feel about messing with hood niggas. They come with jail time, five kids, and three baby mommas. I'm straight."

She was now tryna play a nigga.

"So, why are you sitting here with me?" I came closer to her face, and she tried to move.

"Naw, don't move. Answer me."

"I came because you're no stranger to me. I know the real you and not what the streets say Legend did. That's why I came."

"You still on that old shit I see. I told you I left the streets alone. I'm about to get my construction license back up and running. I'm not on no bullshit with you. I'm too old for this shit. I'm about to be thirty-one."

I had her blushing hard as hell.

"We gone see. Right now, I just want to expand my daycare and focus on stacking my bread."

"That's why I fucks with you. I love a woman that's all about her and her money. That shit is sexy."

"Thanks, Legend. Do you have other females you talk to?" I knew this was coming.

"Naw, I counted on my baby momma to hold me down, but she went ghost. I think her losing our son caused her to give up on us. I haven't heard from her since before I got locked up.

"So, she was the only girl you messed around with?"

"No. I fucked bitches here and there, but it didn't mean shit when I got locked up. I guess it was my fault for leading them on." I grabbed her hand and kissed the back of it.

"Most guys don't even admit to that much. Why you?"

"That's why relationships don't last. These days you gotta keep shit one hundred, especially if it's someone you really like."

———

WE TALKED for a couple more hours while ordering all type of drinks. We had each other laughing like old times. This was the shit I missed the most about us.

"Ok, let me get you home so you can get up for work."

I got up to help her get out of her seat. I left the waiter a tip, and we walked out to the car. It was getting colder, so I pulled her close since she had this little ass jacket on.

Once inside, I really didn't want to let her go. I think my feelings for her had grown even stronger.

"So, can I take you out this weekend and show you some real places Chicago got to offer?" I rubbed her thighs, and that's all it took. She agreed, and I was happy as fuck.

Once I walked her to her door and made sure she locked up, I went home. I didn't want to stick around knowing that my uncle's spirit was all through there. It was creepy as hell. Even though he had his own crib, he still had a lot of his shit in my basement.

The moment I walked into my crib, I felt some cold air come across my face. Once I sat on the couch, I picked up a book that I assumed was my uncle. The title was called *Life After Death*. I felt that he knew he was going to die. I know he is one happy man wherever my uncle went. I poured me a couple of shots and went to my room.

After the funeral, I plan to find me another crib. I got a feeling someone is watching my every move, and I'm not feeling that. I thought when I got inside, I would fall asleep, but when I turned my computer on, I got good news. Since I was on the path of getting my construction license back, I applied for some positions, and my lawyer did as well. I got an email from this guy named Joe. He wanted me to help him out with a couple of projects, and I was all for it. Something is better than nothing until I can get legitimate paperwork and my license. Before I did anything, I made sure my lawyers checked him out. I didn't trust anyone at this moment.

A COUPLE OF DAYS LATER, we were finally laying my uncle to rest. It was hard, but I had to be strong for my family. I was now the man in the family. While I was consoling my sister, Onari walked in and sat next to me. She didn't say anything. She just grabbed my hand, and that's all I needed.

We sat inside the church for two hours before the service was over. The burial was private because we still had no clue who did this to him. I had tried to keep my peace and leave my old life behind, but it was hard. We were inside my cousin's church, and I asked him to pray for me and my sanity. Onari walked up with me, and I suddenly felt like everything would be ok. She held my hand the whole time.

"Your uncle is in a better place. You don't have to dwell on the negative things. He wouldn't want you to be feeling like this," Onari told me while we were getting ready to head to the cemetery.

We all stood around talking about old memories with my uncle until it was time for the gravediggers to lower him. That was the hardest moment of my life.

Walking to where our cars were, I had to thank Onari for being by my side. I reached down and hugged her, and then I helped her in her car.

"Don't forget about this weekend." I forced a smile, and she laughed. I realized I needed to stay occupied to keep from spazzing.

"I got you." I blew her a kiss and watched her leave.

FIVE

NYQUAN WILLIAMS

Walking into my crib, and I could hear my three boys playing the game at four in the morning. They had me fucked up knowing they had to be at school in a couple of hours. My boys were fourteen, twelve, and nine. I had big boys because I started early.

I calmly walked over and turned it off. They knew not to say shit. One thing about me was that I didn't play with them. They were currently staying with me because their mom was in the army. At first, I didn't think I could do it, but I had to support her and step up. It was hard, but I got used to it.

"Its four o'clock and y'all gotta be up in three hours. I don't wanna hear shit when it comes time to wake y'all ass up. Go to bed now."

They each march on up to their rooms, and I went to the basement. I immediately pulled out stacks of money and put it in the safe. The only people who knew where my safe was at was my sister and grandma. If something ever happened to me, I know my kids are gone be straight.

Once I finished, I called over this chick I was messing with named Jory. She was cool as hell, but her brother hated me because I took over his blocks. I never knew she was his brother until it was too late. I couldn't stop fucking with her if I wanted to, so we still be rocking hard.

"Can you come and get me? My car won't start."

"I got you. Be ready."

"Ok."

I hung up and went to pick her up. She didn't live too far, so it only took me about fifteen minutes. Once I pulled up, she was sitting on the porch on the phone. I blew my horn because she didn't see me. Once she got inside, I noticed she was nervous and kept looking behind her.

"Wassup, man. You cool?"

"Yea, I'm just tired." I raised my eyebrow because she sounded like she was tired.

"Man, you better get untired." I began to rub her leg, and she forced a smile.

While riding back to my crib, I noticed a car following me, so I went down side streets to make sure that I wasn't tripping. At the same time, she was texting on her phone and looking out the back window. When I went down the alley, the car followed, and my antennas went up.

"So, you tryna set me up?" My blind eye began twitching, and I pulled my gun out the glove compartment.

"What you talking about?"

I quickly pulled into the back of an abandoned building and snatched her phone. The moment I saw her texting her brother, it was game on.

I placed the gun to her head and blew her brains out. I didn't give a fuck if blood was all over my shit. I then got out and began shooting the car up that was following me. They didn't even see it coming. I shot until I couldn't anymore. I placed my hand inside my hoodie, opened the car door, and found her brother slumped over. His eyes were wide open, so I knew he was dead. I quickly went back, pulled Jory out my car, and left her there. She had me fucked up. I hopped back in the car and pulled away before someone came lurking. I went back home like nothing happened. Now I know I can't trust anyone.

A COUPLE OF HOURS LATER, I dropped my kids off at school, and then my phone began ringing like crazy.

"Bro, you heard what happened?" Legend called me.

"Where you at?" I wasn't about to say shit over the phone

"Getting ready for this class."

"Ok, I'm by yo crib. I'm finna stop through."

"Ok." I quickly met him at his crib and began telling him what happened.

"Bro, that bitch, and her brother tried to set me up. I went to her crib to pick her up, and her brother was following me."

"How you find out?"

"I snatched her phone and seen her text messages. I ended both of them." He just shook his head.

"Now you see why I tell you to watch these bitches?" Legend always told us to keep certain bitches out our circle.

"Where is the gun?"

"I left it inside the car in my garage."

"Ok, I'ma call Duce to get rid of it and have his men to clean the car and get rid of it."

"Thanks, bro."

"No problem. I got you. Just know this my last time helping you. I told you I'm not doing this shit anymore." I didn't like this new Legend. He used to be with all the bullshit.

"Damn bro. It's like that?"

"I told you I'm tryna build a family. I can't go back, or it's over for me. The judge already told me if he sees a third time, he's giving me harder time than before. I can't go back, bro. I wish you get yo shit together."

I ignored him and walked out. One thing I'm not about to do is listen to that bullshit. He didn't call me because he knew when I get pissed ain't no changing my mind. I went back to my sister crib and stayed there until Duce finished.

"Long time no see, big head. Did you hear what happened?" Onari said when she opened the door. She was getting ready to leave out for work.

"Naw, what happened?" I had to play it off.

"Jory and her brother Matthew were killed. They were left behind some abandoned buildings."

"Damn, get the fuck out of here."

"Nope. The police checked his car and found several guns, and lots of drugs, so they think its gang related. Shit is all bad. I'm glad we don't live near that area."

"Wow," was all I said tryna sound like I cared.

"Well, I'm headed out. Be careful in those streets."

"I am. I love you."

"I love you too. Oh, I forgot to tell you someone was hiding in the back seat when Matthew was killed. The police won't reveal who the girl was."

My heart dropped when she told me that shit. It's as if she saw right through my ass.

"Was this on the news?"

"No, they don't want anyone to know because they think the killer will come for her. I heard it from Nastasia. You know they live near the area. I don't know how true it is though."

"Damn, that's fucked up."

"Ok, I'm gone. Grandma fixed breakfast if you want some."

"Ok cool." I watched her get in the car and drive away. I immediately made several calls.

"Yo, I need you to find out if anyone was in the backseat when that happened." I called Duce, and he didn't even have to say much. He was on it.

When I hung up, my grandma's nosey ass was behind me.

"Damn, you scared me."

"You better not be in no shit. Those boys need you."

"I'm not," I said and sat down so that she could fix me a plate. She spoiled us like crazy and still does to this day.

Once I finished eating, I crawled into her bed and was out for the count.

SIX

NASTASIA JACKSON

"Look now, Pike. She said she doesn't want to be with you anymore. You need to leave now."

I was pissed that he was stalking my friend. It was starting to interfere with her work. He was high as hell and constantly scratching like he had a disease. It was too much going on in the streets with Jory and her brother killed. We didn't have time for his shit.

"Or what? You gone call the police?" He was getting bold with those flooding ass pants and long ass socks. Straight clown.

"Nope, I'ma call my brother and my husband," I said, and he got inside a car with some chicks that were enjoying all this shit. He was pathetic as hell riding in a little two-door with about seven people inside. I just laughed.

"It's ok, Nastasia. I can handle him," Onari said, ready to mace his ass. She was with the shits just like me.

When it came to Onari, I didn't fuck around. My brother taught me how to defend myself, and I was ready for whatever. Onari is very quiet, and Pike knew that. One thing I can say is that she wasn't scared of his punk ass. I made sure to inform my boyfriend and brother. This shit was getting out of hand.

"BOOOOOMMMMMM!"

Onari and I looked at each other after hearing a loud noise outside. Luckily, the kids were taking a nap. We both ran outside to find my car window busted. I was beyond pissed now.

"I know that bum ass nigga did that. He'd better go in hiding now." Pike couldn't get to Onari's car because it was parked in the back, so he chose to get at my car.

It took my husband less than five minutes to get here. He came about fifteen deep, including my brother and some chicks that were ready to go to war. After telling them what happened, they were pissed. Legend began making all these calls, and Troy, who is my husband, wanted us to shut it down.

"No, I'm sorry, but I can't just leave my shop because he wants to be an idiot. I've already filed a restraining order against him." Onari wasn't giving up, and I didn't blame her.

"It's cool. Y'all can finish what y'all were doing, and I'ma keep an eye on the place." Legend was trying his best to keep his composure. They surrounded the place and told security to go home because things could get worse.

"You ok, bae?" Troy has always been caring, especially when something was wrong with me. He didn't play that shit.

Troy was a big, chocolate nigga that I fell in love with seven years ago. He was six feet even, about two hundred and fifty pounds, and had long ass dreads down his back. I met him through my brother, and it's been on ever since. It took a minute for me to catch feelings because I've never dated a heavyset guy.

That shit went right out the window when I found out I was pregnant, and then we were soon married. Troy came in and saved me, and I'm grateful for him. My previous boyfriend used to belittle me because I always received compliments, and he didn't like that shit. I stood at five-foot-three, weighed about one hundred and sixty pounds, was light skinned, and had this low fade that I always dyed red or blonde. I didn't fuck around with wigs and weave period. My weight went to my ass and hips, and I was still sexy. As long as he loved me, I didn't give a damn what anyone else thinks.

"I'ma be ok. I think once we clock out, I'ma go home with Onari to make sure that she's ok." He kissed my lips.

"You sure? You know Legend is gone be on that."

"I know. That's my friend, and I want to make sure everything is ok."

"Ok, cool. You know I'ma slide through to check on y'all. Go ahead and get back to work. I don't want y'all stressing. Don't worry about Jr. because I'ma pick him up. I love you."

That's why I loved this man to death.

"Love you too."

I didn't even have to mention my car because he was about to handle that asap. When he and his people walked out, they stayed posted, and I made sure to lock the place up.

WE RESUMED WORK, and when 4:30 came, Onari and I were ready to go get a drink.

"Bitch, I just want to drink, talk shit, and dog Pike's ass out." Onari was getting her coat on while I made sure the cameras were set in every angle of the building.

"I'm with you, but what about Legend? He really likes you."

I really wanted her and Legend to make shit happen. I'm tired of seeing him with a different bitch every day. Since he has been home, bitches have been flocking to him left and right.

"Legend is cool and always has been. I just don't want to fuck up our friendship. I also don't want to deal with someone that's all about the streets."

"I can tell you right now that Legend is getting his shit together. I wouldn't even allow you to fuck with him if he was on some other shit." All the shit Pike did to her has caused her to have trust issues.

"I hear you. Let's roll. I'm ready to drink unlimited wine."

I smiled, and we left out and made sure to lock everything up. We walked around back and just like planned Legend and my husband had niggas everywhere. They trailed us to Onari's crib, and once we got inside, we stripped down to our panties and bra. While I was in the kitchen blending us some fruity drinks, she ordered us some pizza.

"I needed this." Onari began sipping her drinks and had turned to *Good Girls* on Netflix. I popped us some popcorn and had other snacks on deck.

AFTER THREE HOURS OF DRINKING, crying, eating, and laughing, we both were knocked out cold. Luckily, her grandma had Aniyah because we were fucked up.

"Nastasia. Get up. Nastasia." I heard my name and opened my eyes.

"Shit, you scared me, Legend." He had a black bandanna covering his mouth, but I still recognized him.

"How you get in here?" I said, rubbing my eyes.

"Ms. Rosie opened the door for me."

"Aw." I sat up tryna figure out what the fuck he done did. I knew my brother like the back of my hand.

"My fault. I just had to make sure y'all were ok." I knew he was out doing something because he gets all paranoid.

"What did you do, Legend?" I pulled the covers over my body.

"You asking too many questions." He then went to sit by Onari. I just turned back over to go to sleep. I was beyond tired and still drunk off all that wine and fruity drinks.

SEVEN

ONARI

Waking up inside my bed scared the fuck out of me because I know I went to sleep on the couch.

"You hungry?" I heard and jumped up. Legend was holding a plate of eggs, grits, blueberry pancakes, bacon, and a side of orange juice.

"Did you put me in the bed?" I asked while he handed me the food. He sat next to me and smirked.

"Yea, you looked uncomfortable." I started eating my food while he rolled up a blunt.

"You cooked this?"

"Yea. I noticed yo grandma was hungry, so I decided to cook breakfast for her." Legend and my grandma always had a good relationship.

"You remembered I liked blueberry pancakes."

"I know everything about you, Onari. I know what you like and what you don't like. I know yo favorite TV show is *Martin* and you like to eat cookies and cream ice cream. I could go on and on." That shit turned me all the way on.

"Thanks for breakfast." I had to change the subject quick.

"No problem. Eat up so we can get our day started." I forgot about us making plans.

"It's going on twelve. What time should I be ready?"

"You can rest up some more since I got class at one o'clock. Just be ready when I call." He looked tired as hell, which let me know he hasn't been to sleep.

Once I finished my food, I walked him to the door and noticed Nastasia was still knocked out.

"I'ma call you when I'm on my way." He reached down and hugged me.

"You need to start going to bed. You look so tired."

"I know. I've been busy tryna get my business up and running." I smiled because Legend was always into something. I have always been comfortable in front of him. I was in nothing but my bra and panties feeling good.

"Ok, see you later." He kissed my forehead, and I watched him walk to the car. Seeing his men posted out front made me feel a little better.

When he pulled away, I started packing all Pike's shit because it's completely over. It took me a little minute, but when I finished, I climb back in my bed to get some more sleep.

ABOUT FOUR HOURS LATER, I woke up to several missed calls from Legend. I quickly jumped up and spotted Legend and my daughter watching cartoons. He would always ask Nastasia to send him pictures of her and me. It's like he knew everything about her from behind jail.

"You woke, sleepy head?"

"I'm sorry, but I was tired. How long you been here?"

"Not long? Get up and get dressed. Nastasia's gone take her back to her crib since yo grandma is not feeling too good. Is that cool?"

"Yea."

"Ok, we're going downstairs while you get ready."

When he stood up, I noticed he was the shit. He had on a tuxedo jacket with some black jeans and his Stacey Adams shoes. He can dress his ass off.

When they walked out of the room, I jumped in the shower and handled my hygiene. It took me almost an hour. When I finished, I was rocking an all-black dress that I had ordered online. It came just above my knees, not revealing too much. I let my hair fall and put on some black heels, nothing too extravagant.

"Damn ma." Legend was lusting over me hard as hell. I began to blush.

"Ok. Aniyah and I will wait on my hubby to come get us." Nastasia already had her bag packed, so Legend and I walked out.

"Don't forget to set the alarm because grandma doesn't know how!" I yelled to her.

"I know. Have fun and don't make no babies." I just laughed.

Once we got by the car, he opened my door like always. Once we drove off, a car rolled past us, and I could have sworn that I spotted Pike. I wasn't for sure, so I didn't tell Legend. I ignored it because his men were posted around my crib, so I didn't have anything to worry about.

"So, are you gone tell me where we're going?" I smirked because I knew he wasn't gone tell me shit.

"Nope. Just sit back and enjoy." He passed me a blunt, and I got higher than the sky.

When we ended up downtown, I was confused. He pulled directly behind a horse and carriage and got out to greet some white man with a suit. They talked for a little bit, and then he opened my door.

"You ready?"

"Yea." He grabbed my hand, handed the guy his keys, and we climbed inside the horse and carriage. Because it was chilly, we sat inside and not on the top.

"This is so nice, Legend." He grabbed my hand and kissed the back of it. Inside we had all the seafood in the world along with several bottles of wine.

"Anything for you. I noticed you've been unhappy. I don't know why, but you're too pretty to be unhappy. You have to enjoy life for you and Aniyah." He poured me some wine and rolled another blunt.

"How do you know I'm unhappy?" I bit into a big ass shrimp, smacking my ass off. He just laughed because he knows I like to eat. I'm supposed to be eating healthy, but fuck all that.

"What I tell you? I have known you since our teen days, so I know when you're happy or sad. Stop fronting like it's a game." Legend has always been outspoken.

We rode around for two hours enjoying Chicago at night while laughing about old times. He was basically feeding me, and I felt like things were going to another level, in a good way though. He had me blushing like I just met him. I haven't felt this way in so long.

"You ready for the next step?"

"I'm ready." When the ride was over, we went back to the car, and he tipped the guy that was on the carriage with us and the valet driver.

I wasn't sure where we were going, but he made a couple of calls. It only took us about ten minutes for the next destination, which was the W hotel. I didn't ask any questions as to why we were here. I was enjoying myself and didn't want to ruin anything.

"Follow me, beautiful."

He helped me out the car while valet waited to get the keys. Once inside he paid for our room, and it was on from there. Walking into our master suite, it was nice as fuck. He had candles lit, a section set up for massages, and a whole bar.

"You did all this for me?"

"Yep, now get yo robe on so that I can show you want you missing out on."

I was like ok in my head on some kid shit. He poured him a cup of Rémy while I went into the bathroom to undress. When I came out, he had on nothing but his boxers like it wasn't shit, straight chilling.

"Get yo ass over here." He smirked as if he was on some sneaky shit. I walked over and laid across the bed on my stomach.

"Just relax." I did just that.

I relaxed and suddenly felt him pulling my robe up, revealing my ass cheeks. I literally had no panties on. The feeling of his hands and oil made my pussy squirt just a little. He had me in my zone. He began massaging my neck, back, legs, and cheeks. I could feel his dick on brick because he was directly up on me.

It went from that to him pulling my robe all the way off. Again, I had no bra on, so I was completely naked. He poured syrup on my ass, and it was over from there. The moment I felt his tongue please every curve and then my pussy, I screamed silently. I haven't had sex in so long that I didn't know how to react.

He opened my legs wider, and he tongue fucked me so good. I had to grip the sheets to keep from running. It wasn't long before I came all inside his mouth, and he swallowed every drop. He turned me on my back and looked like he wanted more.

"That's how you please yo girl. Now let's enjoy the hot tub." He helped me up, and my legs felt like noodles. He laughed, but on the inside, I wanted more of his tongue.

Once we got inside the hot tub, we just enjoyed each other's company, something most women want and not to have it be all about sex. We stayed up until seven that morning then decided to get some sleep. We both cuddled under each other naked as if we had been doing this.

EIGHT

LEGEND

Waking up and watching Onari sleep like a queen made me smile. I haven't laid up with a bitch in years, let alone get in my personal space. Before I got locked up, I always took a bitch to the hotel, fucked them, and sent them back home. These days bitches have no morals, so I treat them how they want to be treated.

While she was resting, I went down to the gift shop and bought her some flowers and some comfortable clothing and shoes. I also ordered her some food. When I got back to the room, I noticed that I had several missed calls from Duce.

"Yo?" I walked out of the room so that Onari couldn't hear me.

"Bitch, why youp not answering?"

"What's up? I'm with Onari."

"We got a problem?"

"What now? You did handle that, right?"

"Yea, but it's bigger problems. It's true about the back seat."

As bad as I want to say fuck Nyquan, I can't. He lucky he's my homie, but that walking away shit got to stop. He and his brother never want to hear the truth.

"I'm already on it. We gotta get to the bottom of this."

"Bet. I'm on it."

"Ok, cool. Hit me up later."

When we hung up, I went back inside and found Onari in the bathroom brushing her teeth with the robe wrapped around her. I hate I got caught up in his mess, not only that, but we still haven't found out who killed my uncle. Shit was all fucked up. I'm trying not to let this shit distract me from getting my construction license. I was out the other night tryna find out who this girl was in the car. I made sure to cover my face from the cameras in case the police come knocking.

"You hungry?" I asked her when she came out of the bathroom.

She was even prettier when she woke up. She had her hair pinned up, and her thick ass thighs and fat ass had me ready to fuck the shit out of her. I wasn't even planning on eating her pussy, but seeing her pretty pink pearl poking out while I was massaging her ass, made me eat her shit. I couldn't help it. I wanted to fuck her, but she ain't ready for this dick just yet. I just want to take my time with her and show her I'm not just here to fuck. I actually wanted this shit to work.

"Yes, I am hungry."

We both sat down to eat and talk shit like old times. We talked about when we were young, and how I used to stalk her at her job, to me sending flowers that she never got to enjoy because she sent it right back to me.

When we finished eating, we both laid back down and watched movies. Not long after, we got a call saying Nytrell was locked up for tryna steal out of Best Buy. I was pissed.

"I'm so sick of his shit. He is gone stay in there. I'm tired of bonding him out. Nyquan and I told him to get his shit together. He's gone stay in there fucking with me." I could see she was pissed as well. One thing about Onari was that once she helps you and you fuck her over, she's done with you.

"Don't worry. I got him. Let's get our shit on and see what's up."

"No, I'm having a nice time with you." She gave me the sad lips. I just laughed.

"Once I handle this, we are gone spend all day with each other. I'ma bring you to my crib, and we gone finish where we started."

"You lucky I like you, or I would have ended what we started."

"Damn, you cold." She just laughed. Once we took a shower, we both put on our clothes that I got from the gift shop and got out of there.

When we made it to the jail, we found out he not only tried to leave out with three TVs, but he had expensive electronics worth two thousand dollars.

"How did he get the electronics if it's locked up?" Onari asked the officer who arrested him.

"He, Ronald, and some guy named Patrick used plyers and other things to open the cases. The other two got away but we caught him." I was baffled that it was Rondo and Pike with him.

"Are you fucking serious?" Onari was about to go off, but I quickly cut her off.

"We want to bail Nytrell out. How much is his bond?"

"His bond is two thousand, but they added on a thousand for messing the cases up, and for all the items he tried to take, which was twelve thousand." I damn near walked out.

"Ok, we want to bond him out."

"Ok, let me take you to the cashier."

"Ok," I told Onari to stay behind because I had words for his ass.

Once I paid, it took them about thirty minutes to bring him out. When he saw me, he smiled, but I didn't.

"Thanks, bro. I really appreciate it." He tried to shake my hand, and I damn near knock his ass out.

"Fuck that dumb shit. I'm done with yo dumb ass. You out here doing stupid shit like motherfuckers ain't looking out for you. Then you fucking with yo sister baby daddy like he gone help you. That's the end of me fucking with you, and you can forget about coming to her crib. That shit is dead."

He looked like he wanted to cry, but I didn't give a fuck. When he walked out, and Onari went in on him and told him he could no longer stay at the house. He didn't say anything. We dropped him off at Rondo crib, and we left.

As soon as we got to my crib, she got a text from her grandma saying that it was an emergency. We rushed over to her crib.

"Grandma, what happened?"

"I'm missing my twenty dollars. That was my emergency for my medicine."

"When did you notice it was missing?" I asked her.

"I hid it in Onari's room. I checked it right before Nytrell came, and the next day, I noticed it was missing."

I wanted to go off his ass, but I handled it. I gave her my last three hundred in cash, and Onari and I cleaned the place back up.

"Nytrell can't come back here. I know you love him, but this is gone continue if you let it." She said ok, even though I knew she was gone do it anyway.

We decided to make it a family night since shit been fucked up. I went out and got her medicine, and Onari had me pick the baby up since she had been crying. When we made it back, she was cooking some Italian beefs, and grandma was in pain. I massaged her legs after she took her medicine, and the night started. We watched scary movies until we all fell asleep. Aniyah would not let me go, so she slept with me on one of the couches and didn't want Onari to touch me. We all just laughed. I was really attached to them now. I'ma do everything to keep them happy. When I said I wanted a family, I wasn't lying.

NINE

NASTASIA

"Bitch, I know you lying. So you telling me my brother bonded him out for twelve thousand because of all the shit he tried to steal, then he stole from your grandma and was stealing with Pike and Rondo. Oh, you definitely need to let him go his way." I was pissed at what she told me.

"Girl, you know how many times I got him out that jam. I'm done. Legend already told him he had better not come back. He literally stole my grandma's last twenty that she saved for her medicine. She was in pain the whole time."

"God don't like ugly, and he's gone get what his ass deserves."

"Girl, I've been having migraines behind this. Legend literally got up at four o'clock in the morning to get me some pain pills. He even got me some coffee to calm my nerves. I think he's the one."

I began to scream because my brother has been checking for her for years.

"Bitch, I'm so happy. When I tell you that my brother is in love with you, I ain't lying."

"Girl, shut up." We both laughed.

"Don't stress yourself. As long as Legend is around, he's gone make sure you're good."

"I know. It just fucked me up that my own flesh and blood would do that shit to my grandma and me."

"Just know that God don't like ugly."

She nodded her head and finished up our paperwork and began calling the parents that we needed to talk to. Today was Saturday, and on this day, we usually catch up on paperwork.

Once the first parent came in, she immediately walked in and told us she was removing her daughter.

"Ok, but you will need to pay your remaining balance."

"No problem." She had to sign some paperwork before she left.

The next parent walked in with an attitude. She was pregnant and brought her son with her. His name was Patrick as well.

"I'm trying to understand why I'm here." She didn't even sit down. I didn't understand why they were mad at us.

"This baby comes here every morning with dirty clothes on, a snotty nose, no socks, gloves, or hat. It's too cold to have him like that. We can't have him sick around the other kids." I laid it out for her.

"First of all, his dad Big Patrick usually get him ready until I get there. I also have a job I'm trying to keep." That didn't make sense. She didn't even look like she had a job.

"You did just say he get him ready until you get there which means you know what he wears when he leaves out," Onari told her, and she was stuck.

"You know what. I don't got time for this shit." She grabbed her son, and before she walked out, she turned to give us some news.

"Oh, by the way, your daughter will have her second brother." She smirked and walked out. My mouth fell open. Onari didn't look to hurt by this.

"Oh, don't look at me like that. That's their problem, not mine." She smiled, and we both let it go.

I knew he looked familiar. We didn't know because he didn't

have the same last name as Pike. Pike ain't shit, and neither was his Shrek looking bitch.

"Ok, let's get out of here." We packed our bags and got out of there.

Once we got to the car, all of a sudden, a van come speeding and almost hit me, but Onari called my name, and I jumped out the way. I dropped my purse, and the van ran over it and broke my phone. I was literally shaking in my boots.

"Oh my god." I was literally about to cry.

"Rondo."

"Huh?" I asked her.

"I saw Rondo?"

I immediately called my brother and husband off Onari's phone. We stood on the sidewalk until they came. Legend was watching Aniyah, but he took her to our mom and flew over to us.

"Yo, get in the car, asap." Legend was on it. He picked my purse up, and that's when my husband pulled up.

"I saw Rondo," Onari told them, and I could see the veins pop out of Legend's neck. My husband was always calm, but this time he began to make calls, and so did Legend.

"Find Rondo now!" Troy said. We got in the car while Legend had Onari drive her car, and we followed her to his crib.

Once we got to Legend's crib, he went off.

"Are you fucking sure you saw Rondo?"

"Yes," Onari told him.

"We're going to trade y'all cars until we figure it out. In the meantime, I need you to make a police report about what's been going on. Then you need to call the city and have them shut down your daycare temporarily, so they can have those babies put into another daycare," he said and walked away.

Onari looked scared, but she was on it. Troy told her not to mention Rondo's name. I already knew what he was on. It took Legend two hours to cool off.

"I need y'all to get up and let's roll," he said, and we all left out.

We drove to the gun range, and I knew they wanted us to protect ourselves. Legend helped Onari, and Troy helped me.

WE WERE there for almost four hours before we left. I was so tired, I just wanted to sleep. Onari and I picked our kids up from my mom, and we both went home. Legend picked up Ms. Rosie, and they all went back to his house. He wasn't feeling none of what was happening. Once we got in, I received news from my mom that the detective wanted us to meet at his office. It was in regards to my uncle. We put our coats back on and headed to his office. The moment we got there, everybody was sitting waiting on us, and I began to shake for some reason.

"I called you all here to give you an update on your uncle. When we inspected his house for evidence, we found a gray boot, but we couldn't find the other one. Did he own a gray boot?"

"No, he didn't even like the color gray?" my mother told him.

"Do you know who did?"

"No," she told him, and he said some other things while taking notes.

"We also found some bloody money that we know wasn't his blood because we tested it. We will be testing it to see whose blood it was. Give me a couple of weeks, and I will be calling you all."

"We appreciate you," Legend said and got up to walk away.

The whole time we were there, it's like he was in another world. He didn't say anything, nor did he look at the detective. It was something on his mind. I don't know what, but I prayed he didn't get hurt. We all got up to go back home. Once we got in the crib, my husband and I put our son to sleep, and we had a romantic night since my day was fucked up.

TEN

NYTRELL

I was sitting here with a gun in my hand contemplating committing suicide. I literally have no family. I had been sleeping under bridges with blankets, tents, and been getting food from the food pantry. I haven't seen Rondo or Pike in days, and I don't know where he's at. That left me out in the cold. I'm all alone. I don't even have money to survive out here. I was dirty and smelled bad.

Right when I got up, my little brother Nyquan pulled up. He got out and began to beat my ass. I'm talking about stomping me and kicking me all in my head. When he finished, my eye was busted open, and my nose and lips were bleeding.

"The next time you steal anything from my grandma, you dead. You hear me?"

"Yes." I began to spit blood.

"Go yo dumb ass to rehab." He dropped a stack on me and walked away.

I laid there until someone came to help me. It was a nice old lady. She got out her car with a rag and some water. She poured the water on the towel and began to wipe my face.

"Who did this to you?"

"I don't know. It was a random person," I lied. If I told who did this to me, the whole Chicago would be on my ass.

"Let me get you to the hospital."

"No, I'm fine. I just need to get to the rehab center."

"No problem. Let me help you up."

For her to be old, she was strong. She helped me up and walked me to the car. She then grabbed my things and placed them in her trunk. When she took me to the rehab center, she pulled out her business card, and she was a pastor. I knew God was on my side at the moment.

"Thank you so much." She said a prayer with me and then walked me inside. I knew at that moment everything was gone be ok.

She left out, and the receptionist saw my face and called someone. They didn't ask any questions. They took me to the nurse, and she bandaged me up and began asking questions.

"Are you on drugs?"

"Yes, crack."

"Anything else?"

"No." She then asked me about my history and personal information.

I was inside with her for almost an hour, before she took me to this small room with a bed, a small TV, and a bathroom. Before she left, she handed me some pills to start the process of getting clean. I knew if I wanted my family back, I had to get my shit together. She even confiscated the knife I had.

"Dinner is at six, so come down around five forty-five."

"Ok." She handed me some clothes, soap, and other personal items that I needed and walked out.

A WEEK LATER, I was struggling hard, but I was holding on. Every morning, we all get up to eat breakfast and then head to a counseling session to help think of other ways to help with our addiction. Some people walked out because they couldn't do it. Then you had others who helped each other. That's the only reason I didn't give up.

"Nytrell, you have a pass for five hours. You must be back in time, or that's a write-up."

"No, thank you."

She smiled, handed me some books and a cup of coffee before leaving. This is supposed to help you, but it hasn't done anything to me yet. I stayed inside my room and began looking at the books. When neither of them caught my attention, I began drawing, which was one of my passions. I could also paint my ass off. When I got deep into it, I got a knock on the door.

"Yea?" It was the guy that stayed next to me.

"I wanted to see if you wanted to play Spades. I notice you barely come out of your room."

I thought about it then told him yea. I grabbed my coffee and headed to the activity room. We played cards all the way until it was lunchtime. I actually had a nice time with him and two others.

"If you ever wanna get out the room, don't hesitate to knock on either of our doors. By the way, my name is Jack, and this is Charles and Mason."

"Thanks' y'all. I'm Nytrell."

When we finished eating, we were free to do whatever. I went back to my room and turned to the news. The first thing that caught my attention was a picture of Jory and her brother Matthew. Word around town was that she and her brother Matthew were setting people up to get robbed. Jory had been messing around with my brother for years on and off. I'm starting to think it was a setup. That's fucked up what happened to them. The second story almost made me throw up.

They announced a man was hanging from a tree with his neck broke from the large rope. When they showed the picture, it was

Rondo. I covered my mouth. I knew it was the work of Legend, Duce, and Troy. I began to throw up because I knew they probably found out what we did. I just hope he didn't mention me. I stayed up all night tryna figure out how they found out, or if this was related to what we did.

WHEN THE SUN CAME UP, I got a knock on my door saying that breakfast was ready. I played sick and had them bring my food. Of course, the nurse came to check on me. I played like I had stomach problems. Because I was recovering, I couldn't take medicine, so she brought me some soup, and crackers, and gave me some orange juice.

Later that day, I had to come down, but they didn't tell me why. Once I got to the lobby, it was my grandma and Onari.

I stood there for a minute before my grandma came to hug me. She began to cry, and I felt bad. I've been causing her all this pain when she stepped up to take care of us. I walked them to the sitting area so that we could talk.

"I'm so sorry for what I put y'all through." I hung my head, and Onari gave me a hug as well.

"I don't want to bury you, Nytrell. I don't. I buried your mom and dad, and I almost committed suicide. I want y'all to bury me," she said, wiping her eyes. I felt her pain.

"I just want you to get out and do right. It's too much going on in the streets." Onari started crying, and I couldn't take it. My eyes began to water, so I grabbed the tissue.

"I'm trying y'all. It's hard."

"We're here to help you. You gotta stay strong and fight it." My grandma placed her hand on my shoulder.

After all the crying, we got up to go to the game room. That's when they told me Rondo was killed, and I told them I saw it on the news. It was silent for a minute before I changed the subject.

"Let's play Spades."

"Let me tear you up like old times."

Onari was ready, and grandma was already talking shit. We played for two hours before it was time for them to leave. When I went back to my room, I actually slept well knowing that my family didn't give up on me.

ELEVEN

NYQUAN

I had been running around doing all type of shit, and I haven't spent time with my kids, so today I decided to take them out.

"Where do y'all wanna go today?"

"Out to eat and to the arcade."

"Ok, deal. Get dressed so we can go."

They all got ready within thirty minutes, and then we headed to a wing place. One thing about my boys was that they didn't care about expensive foods. They wanted simple things like eating chicken and other simple foods.

When we got to the restaurant, my youngest Nasir began asking questions about Nytrell. I didn't want to respond, but I knew how much he loved Nytrell.

"Right now, he's somewhere getting back right. He wants to get himself together so that he can spend time with y'all."

They didn't ask another questioned. We changed subjects and started talking about my oldest son Nathan birthday.

"What you wanna do for your big day?"

"I just want mom to come home." He was the quiet one and was crazy about their mom.

"You know she won't be home for another two months." I felt bad because they always wanted her to be around. They knew she was doing it for them.

"How about this, what if I took you, your brothers, and two of your friends on a plane ride to Miami so that we can get out of this cold Chicago weather?"

They all jumped for joy, and I smiled. I knew that would do it.

"Let's eat."

We ate and then went to the arcade. Once we got inside, they all started making bets for big money. I just laughed because I missed times like this with my boys. Even though I was in the streets, my boys were my first priority. They gave me hope that I would one day get out of the game.

We played in the arcade until it closed and I lost almost ten thousand, but they knew they would never see that much. Once we got home, they knew the drill. They jumped in the shower and went to bed.

My next step was going to see about the girl that was supposed to had been in the backseat when everything went down. Her name was Bianca and she had run her mouth to so e locals, which let me know she probably informed the police as well. I didn't even tell Legend. I wanted her all to myself.

———

ONCE I PULLED UP, I got out and knocked on her door. She didn't even ask who I was. She was shocked when she saw it was me.

"You wasn't expecting me, huh?" I pushed the door open and walked right in. She pissed on herself and began begging me not to kill her.

"Please, don't hurt me. Please."

"Calm down. I'm here to negotiate some things." I sat at the table and rolled me a blunt.

"I want you to act like you didn't see a thing. You don't know me, and it wasn't me. Can you do that?"

"Yes. Yes, I can."

"I will give you ten grand, half now and half later." Her eyes lit up, and I knew my job was done.

"Ok, I don't know you."

"Good. The first half will be sent to you in a week," I said and walked out. I wanted to make sure that she wasn't on anything sneaky.

After leaving, I went to my homie's crib to chill and watch them play cards for money, something we always do. As soon as I walked inside, I spotted Pike and some other guys talking about Legend. I didn't really fuck with Pike because of the shit he put my sister through. One thing I never do is interfere with her relationships, which is why we taught her how to throw them hands.

"That nigga is a straight clown now. All of a sudden, he gets out and is on some family type of shit. The whole time he was in there, he kept saying we gone get back on top," one guy name Fish said.

Before Legend went away, everybody ate. No dope boy out there went hungry. He fed families who didn't have food and helped the homeless. When he got locked up, workers turned to stealing, robbing, and other illegal means to survive. Others got on drugs, and some died from it.

I did the smart thing. All the money I had, I tripled and rebuilt what he started. The only thing is, when he was out, every one of our blocks did at least ten thousand a day. Now I can barely get five in.

"I think if we get rid of him, things will go back to normal," Pike said, and I knew right there he was tryna get himself killed.

"Y'all must haven't heard about Rondo?" I didn't even have to say what happened because it was all over the news. If they knew what I knew, they wouldn't dare fuck with him. He might be kind to a lot of people, but deep down Legend was a demon.

They all got quiet and continued to play cards. After a couple of drinks, and a plate of food, I got right out of there.

A COUPLE OF DAYS LATER, I went to see Nytrell. I felt bad as hell, but he deserved it. To go and steal from my grandma was some fucked up shit, not to mention he was out there wilding with Rondo and now Pike started fucking with them. I wasn't feeling that.

"What's going on? How is everything coming?" I asked him when he came down.

"It's all good." He seemed nervous, so I eased him up a little.

"I'm glad you still in here tryna get yo shit together. I don't ever want you to think what I did was from hate. It's all love. I don't want what happened to Rondo to happen to you," I said, and he nodded his head.

"Thanks, bro. I know I fucked up too many times, but I will not go back down that road. I never want to lose my family." I gave him a hand pound, and I could see in his eyes that he was going to be ok.

"What's been going on in here?" I could see he gained a little weight while being in here, which was a good thing.

"I started going to church a week ago and got baptized to cleanse my soul. I did something that will eat me up for the rest of my life." His eyes got cloudy, but he wiped them before the tears fell.

"Care to share?"

He hesitated and then finally went into details.

"Pike, Rondo, and I were tryna get some money to get our drugs, so Pike decided we could rob Legend's uncle since we knew he had a safe inside his house. We thought he was gone since his car wasn't outside. I used a safety pin to get inside the front door, and when we got inside, things went bad. We all looked around, and out of nowhere, he came out of with a gun and tried to shoot, but Rondo was faster. He shot him and killed him. They came back out, and I was told Rondo shot him. We didn't know he was inside, and the plan was never to kill him."

When he finished, I damn near choked. Now I know why Rondo was probably killed. Legend never disclosed what he does in the streets, but I knew it was him and because of what happened to his uncle.

"Fuck man! What the fuck were you thinking?"

He didn't say anything, so I walked out before I beat his ass again. When I left, I was tryna find a way to keep this information from leaking, which meant I had to find out what Legend knew.

TWELVE

LEGEND

After that shit with Rondo, I knew shit would slow down. Niggas knew my mark, so I'm sure they knew it was me but wouldn't dare say a word. When the detective told me what type of shoe it was, I knew it was him. Then the fact that he tried to run my sister and Onari over had me pissed. He had to go. Now, I'm tryna figure out who was with him when that shit went down with my uncle, and I won't stop until I find them.

"You woke?" Onari asked me while lying on my chest.

Since all of this shit died down, I was able to spend a lot of time with her and Aniyah, while going to school and doing other things to benefit us. The only thing I didn't like was that they had gone back to the house. I begged her to come stay with me, but that didn't work. My only other option was to buy a big ass condo for us all and leave that shit there.

"I'm up thinking."

She sat up and asked me, "What's wrong?"

"I'm just thinking about everything that's been going on, and how I want to do right by you and build a family." She blushed like always.

"I've been thinking the same. I just want us to take things slow and build a relationship."

"Let's start then."

"We already did," she said, and I laughed.

We stayed up all night, forgetting that I had school and she was going to get her hair done for our weekend vacation, which was Valentine's Day, and my birthday was the following day.

"Where are you going?" She got out the bed with her robe wrapped around her body.

"To fix you breakfast. Get some sleep and don't worry about what I'm doing," she said tryna get smart. I smirked and got me about three hours of sleep before she woke me up.

"It's ready," she said and got my clothes ready. I always wanted this shit.

"I'm going back to the house once I finish getting my hair done."

"Ok. When I leave school, I'm going to help this man with fixing up this house, so I should be home by nine. Is that ok?"

I always inform her of my whereabouts and ask her about the time of me coming in. My uncle taught me everything I know, so keeping her happy wasn't too hard. That always keeps your woman at ease.

"That's ok. I'ma have dinner ready and something sexy on."

My dick immediately went up. She laughed hard as hell, but she better not play with me. I had been sleeping in the bed with her for almost three weeks, and every night I be wanting to fuck her in her sleep.

"Yo, don't play with me. I just might leave early on dude ass."

"Go to school, Legend." She walked off tryna avoid what I was saying.

Once I washed up and got dressed, she handed me my food and I kissed her juicy lips then walked out.

When I made it to class, I partnered up with this chick that I knew was feeling me, but I wasn't feeling her and wouldn't dare fuck over Onari. She kept grabbing my shoulder thinking that it was ok, but I checked her quick.

"You cool and all, but I don't allow anyone to touch me." Her face went red, but that was the truth, especially if I didn't know you.

"I'm sorry," she said, and we began working on our assignment. We then went out to start getting our hands dirty.

———————

MY CLASS WAS over two hours later. I then went to help the guy out with the crib, and that's when I got tired. I helped him knock walls down and other things that were inside the crib. When we finished, we had to cover the outside because of the cold weather.

"I'ma send your check to your bank," he told me, and I shook his hand. He was teaching me a lot, and I really appreciate it. After checking his background, we found out he was legit.

When I made it to Onari's crib, she had my food hot and ready, a blunt rolled up, and my bottle of water. We all ate together just like we did growing up.

"You look gorgeous," I told her. She had gotten her hair flat ironed with a little color.

"Thanks." She quickly changed the subject.

"So, I forgot to tell you Pike had a baby that I never knew about, and now he has another baby on the way. The baby was in my class-room this whole time."

That didn't sit right with me. I'm always overthinking things, and that sounds like a setup.

"How long has he been in there?"

"About nine months now."

"You need to change whatever paperwork you think Pike may know about. I don't trust that at all." She agreed with me, and when she finished eating, she began making calls.

When I finished, I grabbed Aniyah and put her to sleep. She was nodding off at the table. Once she was all the way sleep, I jumped in the shower, and before I knew it, I was knocked out cold.

A COUPLE OF DAYS LATER, I was happy because it was our little getaway for the weekend. I had been working on that house and going to school for my hours. I was beyond tired, but now I'm excited about what I had in store for her.

"We're coming back," I told Aniyah who was crying her eyes out because we were leaving. She was reaching for me, so I turned to her favorite song. Once that scary sound came on, she looked around at all of us and then slowly stopped crying. When the words started, she began to dance and clap her hands, and we all laughed.

"You think you got her for a whole weekend?" Onari asked her grandmother, and she told us to go head before Aniyah sees us leave.

I kissed her cheek, and we walked to the car. I had a funny feeling someone was watching us leave, so I made sure that someone was on standby to keep them safe.

WE DROVE ALMOST two hours to a quiet resort where we had a big ass cabin, filled with everything we needed. We didn't have to go out for anything. Plus, the weather was bad where we were going.

"Where do you see yourself in the next five years?" she asked me out of nowhere while rolling my blunt.

"In five years, I see myself with kids of my own, a bigger house, traveling the world to exotic places, but most of all, I see myself marrying you," I said while rubbing her thigh.

"You're too perfect." She began to giggle, and her face turned red.

"What about you?"

"I just want to live a happy, peaceful life with you, Aniyah, and everyone else in my family. I don't care about other things. I just want to wake up every morning knowing my family is ok."

I couldn't help but pull over. I grabbed her face and gave her nothing but this tongue. We kissed for almost two minutes before we heard beeping. I looked back, and it was the police.

She panicked, but I didn't.

"How are you doing?" I asked a white male cop.

"I stopped you because your brake lights are broken." I frowned.

"I'm sorry, sir, but I didn't realize it."

"It's fine. How far are you to your destination?"

"About thirty more minutes." He seemed cool.

"Ok, get there and get it fixed. If you get pulled over, let them know Officer Ware already pulled you over."

"Thanks. I really appreciate it." He nodded and walked away.

Onari could see I was pissed about my lights. When I got out to check it, someone had broken the right rear lights and then left a note halfway sticking out the trunk.

I'ma get my bitch back one way or another.

I knew it was Pike.

"Come on. Let's not make this weekend horrible." Onari got out the car and kind of calmed me down. We got back inside and quickly got to our destination.

"Oh my god, it is so pretty. Look at the whole place lighting up!"

She was like a kid in the candy store. When I pulled up to the driveway and got out, some lady came out and handed us a welcome basket.

"Thanks, Mulu." I handed her a twenty, and she tried to help us with our bags.

"Oh, no. Ladies never carry bags. I got this." She smiled then turned to Onari.

"You're a lucky woman to have him. I hope you two enjoy your vacation," she said and got inside her car.

"You go inside and get sexy for me," Onari smirked and walked up the stairs.

Once I finished grabbing our bags, I walked into an amazing cabin. They had all kinds of stuff for us. While I was getting everything set up, I quickly made a phone call to one of my private investigators. I needed to know where the fuck Pike was at.

"Ready?" I heard and looked up.

"Damn, girl." I set my phone down and ran up the stairs to rub all over her bare ass. She had nothing on but her red bottoms, and a G-string. Tonight, was about to be epic.

THIRTEEN

ONARI

I just knew that when we got here, everything would be ok. The shit Pike pulled, Legend will never let it go. The fact that he is trying everything in his power to bring us down is sad. I just hope he doesn't get killed behind everything's he's doing. Right now, I'm trying to keep him sane because I know he is thinking of ways to hurt him.

I didn't expect things to go this fast with Legend and me. It's like he's too perfect with everything he does. Every morning he makes sure that he does something to keep a smile on my face. When he went to freshen up, I poured me some wine, and him some Rémy and waited on him to return. Thirty minutes later, he came down with nothing on but his robe and a big massage kit.

"Thanks, ma," he said when I handed him his drink. He then instructed me to lie on the couch face up. He opened up some different oils and began pouring it on my body.

"OMG, this feels so good!" I said, closing my eyes.

I could smell the sweetness of the oils. He started on my feet first then made his way up to my titties. He used a wet cloth to wipe the oil off, and then I suddenly felt his lips around my nipples. He was slowing sucking them, which almost made me cum. This was my spot, and I don't understand how he knew it.

"You got a nigga sprung. I don't know what you did to a nigga, but I will never let you get away from me." I looked into his eyes, and couldn't help but smile.

When he finished sucking my nipples, he went down to my pussy and raised my legs as far as they would go. The moment his tongue entered my pussy, I damn near screamed for him to stop. That's how good it was.

"Legend! Oh my god! This shit feels so fucking good!"

He was sucking my pearl softly until precum began oozing out, then he went down and stuck his tongue inside my pussy while playing with my nipples. I grabbed hold of the back of his head and all of a sudden, my juices came running out at full speed.

"I LOVVVVEEEE YOOOOOUUU SOOO MUCH!" I screamed so loud that I know the people in the next cabin heard me.

"I knew you did. I love you too, girl," he said while smiling and wiping his mouth.

"Now, let me make love to your whole body." He stood and took off his robe.

When I say I almost ran out of there because this nigga had a curve in his dick, I ain't lying. Not only that, but he had an anaconda. His dick was so big, I knew that I would never be able to deep throat his shit.

"Don't worry. I won't hurt you." I was speechless, and he found it funny. I just closed my eyes and let him do what he wanted.

He put my legs on top of his shoulders, and when he began to enter me, I tried to hide the pain.

"Damn, girl. When was the last time you had sex?" He was having a hard time, so he grabbed some sex oil, and rubbed it all over his dick.

"Ahhhh!" I said under my breath when he finally got the whole thing in. It was so tight that it felt like my skin was peeling on the inside.

"Fuck man," he moaned while his eyes were closed. About five minutes in, it started to feel good as hell.

"Ohhh Legend, it feels so good. I love you so much."

"I love you too, baby. Oh my fucking god." He began fucking me faster, and we both went nuts, calling each other names and kissing like crazy.

"Look at me when I'm fucking you," he demanded.

"I can't. It feels so good." That curve in his dick was hitting spots that I never knew existed.

"What the fuck I say?" I just couldn't.

"OOOOHHHHHH!" His powerful dick had my juices running like water coming out the faucet.

"Now, turn yo ass around." I always loved the dirty talk during sex, so I was ready for whatever.

"This is my pussy now." He smacked my cheeks, and then I suddenly felt his tongue in my ass hole. This the first time I ever got my ass ate, and it felt great.

"Legend, what are you doing to me?"

"I'm making you all mines— forever," he said and began doing something I never knew my body could.

After eating my ass for almost three minutes, I suddenly felt something coming out. At first, I thought it was shit, and got scared. When it all came out, I touched it, and it was cum. I didn't even know cum could come out the ass.

Oh, he wasn't done. He entered my pussy from behind and began slowly fucking me, causing me to grab hold of the couch. I damn near broke my nails trying hold on. He fucked the shit out of me, causing tears to come down my eyes. I haven't had sex in so long, and I was about to become a sex addict.

"You love me, right?" he asked me while grabbing ahold of my neck.

"Yesssss!" I moaned.

"Then say it." He began to grunt like he was about to cum.

"I love you, Legend. I love you so much. I always have."

"I love you too, Onari."

"Fuuuucck!" He came on all inside of me, and I came right after. He pulled out and collapsed on top of me catching his breath

"Damn seven years without sex is a motherfucker."

We cuddled for ten minutes before we got up to shower together. Once we finished, Legend went downstairs to cook us some food while I got in the bed to find us a movie to watch.

Once he came up, he sat down a big pan of all type of seafood. It was definitely a seafood boil.

"I'm about to smash this," I said, and he laughed. He knew how much I loved seafood. He then handed me a water bottle, napkins, and anything else I needed.

"What movie do you want to watch?" I asked him, and he said something scary. I should have already known that.

"I'ma pick *Texas Chainsaw Massacre*. Did you see this already?"

"Naw. What's it's about?" He started eating his food.

"Just watch it. It's crazy as hell." I put it on, and we began watching it and eating our food.

"Awwww, hell naw. No, the fuck he didn't. Bae, he's about to kill all of them," I said while wiping my mouth.

"Dude is dumb as fuck. How you let him get to you when he was miles away?" I agreed with him. We talked through the whole movie, cussing them out like they could hear us.

"Yea, that was a good ass movie."

He began grabbing our empty plates and cleaning everything up. This time I picked a movie on Lifetime that I know he would like. Legend is not the average person. He likes all kinds of things. There are very few men who like Lifetime movies, and he is one of them.

When he came back up, he climbed in the bed, and I laid on his chest.

"So, I've been thinking about what we got going on. Like I'm scared, but at the same time, I wanna give this a try. I just don't want no secrets or anything popping up that will hurt me." I finally told him what was on my mind.

He pulled me closer and kissed my forehead.

"The first time my sister brought you around, it was something about you. I never could figure it out until we had a party and you came. Every female at the party was half-dressed, and some was checking for all the niggas in there, not you though. You weren't half-dressed, and you sat in the corner drinking your wine and smoking your weed. That's what attracted me to you. I had never seen that before in Chicago."

He then sat up and grabbed both of my hands.

"I don't ever want you to think I will hurt you. In all of my years on earth, I have never hurt a female before because when I start talking to a girl, I let her know what the deal is up front. If I'm fucking different bitches, that means I have no title with them, and they all understood from the beginning. With you, it's different."

"How?"

"You're the first female that ever made me feel some type of way. I've never had feelings with anybody else. It gives me life every time I see you. I love you, no bullshit. As far as secrets, there are no secrets because you know everything about me. I just want you to trust me. I'm trying to build a family with you and Aniyah. Are you willing to go all the way with me?"

"Yes."

He pulled me in and began giving me the nasty kiss that makes yo panties wet.

"Now get ready because when we get back home, I'm buying us a new house that you will pick out. Yo grandma will be coming as well."

I didn't even argue. I told him ok, and we finished watching the movie.

THE NEXT MORNING, he surprised me with a dozen roses,

scented candles that I loved so much, different types of candy, wine, weed, and some keys.

"Happy Valentine's Day, baby."

I almost cried because I never got a gift from a boyfriend on that day. My father was the only man that ever gave me a gift.

"Thank you so much." I hugged him, and he told me to look out the window. When I opened the blinds, I saw a big ass red 2019 Escalade. The exact same truck I have been looking to buy for myself.

"No, you didn't!" I covered my mouth and jumped up and down.

"I love you so much. Now get rid of both those cars. You don't need them."

"I love you too."

When the shock was over, he catered to me for the whole day. We had sex all over again, we played games, ate, play fought, and lots of other things.

"Let's play Deuces for money?" I said while grabbing some cards.

"Ok, ten dollars a game." This was something he loved to do.

"I only got debit," I said, laughing hard as hell.

"How are you gone play then?" He had a smirk on his face.

"With yo coins, now let's roll." He busted out laughing, and so did I.

"You a fucking clown, man," he said, handing me a stack.

About an hour in, I was winning all his money. He was losing so bad that he smoked about four blunts before he quit.

"Here," I gave it all back, and he frowned.

"Why you give it back?"

"Because my money is your money," I told him and gave it back.

"It's yours then. Now let's fuck again."

I knew this was going to happen, which is why I was glad I had soaked in some water. I guess he was releasing seven years of built up nut.

"Let's do it," I said, and we both laughed. All day we played games and fucked off and on, something that I could definitely get used to.

FOURTEEN

NASTASIA

After everything that happened, my husband wasn't for none of the foolishness. I couldn't leave out of his sight. We went everywhere together, and we made sure he was always loaded with his guns. I was scared as hell because I heard Nytrell left the rehab center and was back on drugs. He was robbing any and every one he could think of with Pike. The crazy part is I knew my brother was looking for him, and he could never be found.

"I want to send you and my son away from here. Things are about to get bad, and I don't want y'all to get hurt."

Troy was already on the internet booking us a flight. I knew I couldn't protest this, so I started packing although I didn't even know where I was going.

"You wanna go to Jamaica?" he asked me while drinking his beer.

"Yes. I haven't been there in years." I got excited now because when Onari and I went, we had a blast.

"Ok, start packing. Onari and everyone else in the family will be down there as well. Don't tell anyone, especially over the phone, not even to Onari because Legend wants to surprise her." He had everything planned out.

It took me almost three hours to pack everything because I didn't know how long we would be staying. Once I finished, we left and went to get my son from my mom's house. I waited there for my mom to finish getting ready while she was on the phone.

"Girl, you know we're going to Jamaica? Girl, yea, my son paid for the whole family to go. It's some shit going on in those streets, and I'ma find out and get my Glock ready to start bussing." She was telling everything like they didn't tell her to keep it a secret.

"Mom, what are you doing?" I grabbed the phone and hung up.

"Damn, that was my friend." She rolled her eyes, and I gave it back.

"They don't know what's going on, which is why you shouldn't be saying anything." She just walked away and finished packing her things. Once she finished, we met everyone at the airport but was almost late because she had to get some cigarettes. Onari's daughter and grandma were there as well.

The only thing I wanted to do was sleep. I've been feeling overwhelmed about a lot of things, mainly my husband and brother getting killed.

"How are you feeling?" I asked Ms. Rosie because when she found out Nytrell was out, she broke down crying. I think she knew he would never get back on the right track.

"I'ma be ok. I've been through worse situations." I hugged her, and she smiled.

Once we went through the checkpoint, we all boarded the plane, and I immediately went to sleep. Hours later, we were landing, and when everyone got their things, we got into a taxi and went to the hotel. I was glad we were in the heat and out of the cold. My bones don't work with that type of weather.

"Ohhh. Look at the trees. This place is amazing," Ms. Rosie said while taking pictures. I was glad she was smiling now.

As soon as we got inside our rooms, Onari came an hour later, and we began to plan what we were going to do for that day.

"BITCH, YOU BETTER NOT FALL!" I yelled at Onari while all of us, even my mom and Ms. Rosie, were skating. We all were holding on to each other while laughing.

"Bitch, it's too slippery."

"It's supposed to be," I said trying not to go down. In this moment, we all could forget about the things we've been going through. We skated for an hour and then went to get something to eat. We went to a Jerk spot and damn near ate until we passed out.

"Girl, I'm stuffed," Onari said when we got back to the hotel. She was knocked out in my room, and I went to sleep right behind her.

"ONARI. NASTASIA. GET UP." I opened my eyes, and Ms. Rosie was standing over us.

"What's wrong?" I could see that she had been crying.

"It's my brother. He had an asthma attack and is now fighting for his life. I need to get to him asap," she said, and we both jumped up ready to pack our things.

"No, stop. I want you two to stay here like they told y'all, and I will go alone. I already booked my flight back."

We knew we couldn't argue with her, so we helped her pack her things. I knew how close she and her brother were so I know she was hurting bad. When we finished helping her, we called a cab to take her to the airport.

"I'm so tired of all the bad things that have been going on. It's like one minute things are good, then the next everything come crashing down on us," Onari said with tears in her eyes. I just hugged her like I always do.

She and her daughter stayed in my room for the rest of the night, and we watched movies all night long.

WE'VE BEEN in Jamaica for a full week, and we haven't heard anything from Ms. Rosie, Troy, or my brother. We were starting to get worried.

"Do you think we should call them?" I asked, and Onari told me no.

"I think we should call the hospital to see if she made it." Onari picked up the hotel room phone and called there.

"Hi, I was calling to see if Rosie Williams came to visit her brother by the name of Charles Williams. My name is Onari Williams," she told the person on the other end of the phone.

"I'm sorry, but we don't have a Charles Williams. The lady already came, but she left. This was about four days ago." My heart dropped when she said that.

"Are you sure?" Onari asked her with tears coming down her face.

"I'm positive. We have a small hospital, and I can see every name we have here, including family members' names as well."

"Ok, thanks."

"Oh my god, please let my granny be ok!" Onari screamed, and the trip was over. I didn't care what they said.

We began packing our things hoping everything would be ok and she would be at home. We left some of our things at the hotel to get to her. As long as we got the most important things, we didn't care. I cried half the way home just praying.

FIFTEEN
NYTRELL

"Damn bro, save me some," Pike said while I was embracing my body with the best crack they invented.

"Here." I handed him what was left.

"Bro, you know what we gotta do next, right?" he asked me.

"We gotta go harder. Our next mission is to go get grandma," I said, not having a care in the world.

The way Nyquan walked away from me let me know my family will never fuck with me again. Me telling him what I did was a way for me to get over it and get my life together. Things didn't happen like I planned, so I'm at a point now that I don't care if I die.

"Yes, and I'ma make her pay for what Legend did to Rondo," Pike said, and I agreed.

I had already called the hotel like I was a hospital worker and lied about her brother having asthma, and she believed it. Now we're waiting for her to get here. Legend thought he was slick and had the locks changed, so Pike got us inside his way. We waited already knowing she would come home to call out on her house phone. My grandmother never had a cell phone and didn't believe in them. She says the government is monitoring everything we do. We had a full course meal and drunk some of her beers just because before we got high. I knew no money was in the house because Legend supposedly put everything in the bank.

"I hear the keys in the door," Pike said, and we both ran to get in the closet. I'm glad I cleaned up the mess we made, except the kitchen area, which is where we will attack her from behind.

"Legend something is going on. I got a call telling me my brother had an asthma attack. I just called him, and he is fine," I heard her say. I peeked out, and she was on the phone.

"Get out of there now," he said calmly as hell. She talked to him for a couple more seconds and then hung up. He told her to leave, so we came out the closet before she could make it to the door.

"Where the fuck are you going?" I grabbed her from behind while Pike got the ropes to tie her up.

"Oh my god," she said scared as hell. I threw her on the floor, making her hit her head.

"AHHHHH!" she yelled, while we both tied her hands to the table.

"Damn, grandma. You heavy as hell." I laughed then sat down to catch my breath.

"Why, Trell? Why would you do this to me?" She began crying trying to get her hands untied.

"That ain't gone work," I said, referring to her trying to get loose.

"You never did love me, none of y'all. Ever since I was little, you've always overlooked me and focused on Onari and Quan. All I ever wanted was for you to love me. I blame you for why my life took a bad turn." I started getting emotional because this is how I been feeling for years.

"Why would you say that? I love all three of you equally. I have never picked over anyone of you."

"Yes, you did. You started loving me when the doctors told you I almost died from pneumonia."

I picked up my gun and Pike did what he came to do. I didn't have time to talk with her. She didn't beg or anything. She began reciting prayers while Pike began to have sex with her. I turned my head until he finished.

"I'm done."

When he pulled his pants up, I raised the gun and shot her in her head with no remorse.

"Now, who's next," I said and blew smoke with my mouth from the gun. With blood oozing out, I knew she was dead.

THE NEXT DAY, Pike and I were on a mission. I'm talking about harassing everyone to find Legend. I knew Onari and everyone else was probably on their way back to Chicago, so we were planning to give them special treatment. The crazy part about all of this was that Legend, Troy, and Duce was nowhere to be found. Nobody in the streets wanted to tell us where they would be.

"I heard y'all were looking for Legend," this girl walked up to me and said. She looked very familiar, but I couldn't put my finger on it.

"Where?"

"He's sitting at the bar on Taylor Street," she said and walked away. I knew she wasn't lying because that's where he goes to unwind.

The moment we got to the bar, I didn't see anyone of them. I checked the bathrooms, the other side of the bar, and the parking lot hoping that they didn't leave.

"FUCK!" Pike yelled.

"We need a new strategy to get to them. I can't let them get to me because I already know the outcome. Even though I don't care, we need to figure this shit out," I said and we started walking down the street.

POW! POW!

I heard gunshots and suddenly felt a sharp pain in both of my legs. The same thing happened to Pike.

"Ahhhhhh!"

I looked up and spotted Legend in a black truck. He didn't blink, nor did he get out to come towards us. That's when I knew he was playing mind games. He was skilled at plotting, especially when it comes to killing someone.

"Are you guys ok?" the owner of the bar and a couple of others came to check on us. I wasn't no snitch, so we declined the offer for them to take us to the hospital.

"We ok. We gone take ourselves."

With blood leaking out our legs, we both struggled to get up, even though we were in a lot of pain. Luckily, we were near an abandoned spot that we sleep in from time to time. Once we got inside, we both sat on the floor and began wrapping our legs with some clothing that was left behind.

"I hope they didn't see us coming in here," I

said. I know I fucked up now that Legend saw me.

"You do know if they wanted us, they would have got us. Legend doesn't care about anyone being around." I knew he had some type of plan to get rid of us.

"Fuck that nigga."

Pike was trying his best to wrap his legs while struggling. This shit was painful as hell. Luckily, I had pain medicine and our second dose of crack to keep us going. Once everything kicked in, we both nodded off, and I started feeling the pain fade away slowly.

"AAAHHHHH!" I screamed but couldn't move. The feeling of something burning my skin made me open my eyes.

Standing over me was Troy and Duce. Duce was an animal just like Legend. I said a prayer because I knew I was going to hell for all the wrong I did. Legend was sitting in a chair with eyes as cold as ice while smoking a blunt. They each were holding a chain saw, and a blowtorch.

"You ready to meet your maker, bitch?" Duce said. I closed my eyes when he raised the chainsaw.

"No," I heard Legend say and opened my eyes.

"I wanna save him for last. Let's get this faggot nigga who likes to rape old women and shoot them." I looked over, and they had Pike hanging from the ceiling upside down naked.

"I want you to watch what we gone do to you when we finish with him."

I shitted and pissed on myself when I saw them take the blowtorch and burn his dick to a crisp. It literally fell off. I can't even tell y'all the screams he made, and then he passed out.

SIXTEEN

NYQUAN

This morning, I woke up with a funny feeling, a feeling that caused me to pack my kids' things and send them to their godmother's house. She didn't live too far, so I got them there in a heartbeat.

"Call me when y'all get inside. I'ma be back in a couple of days to get y'all."

"Ok. Love you, dad," they all said together.

I pulled away and decided to bring Bianca the other half of the money for keeping her mouth shut. It's been a week since I gave her the first half, and I haven't heard a thing from the police. As soon as I made it to her crib, I could see she was standing on the porch. I got out, and she let me into her crib.

"Good job for keeping your mouth shut," I smirked and handed her an envelope with her money inside.

"Just know that I will always keep my eyes on you." I winked at her and then walked out. I wasn't playing when it came to shit like this. She nodded then let me out.

As soon as I got to my car, police cars came flying at full speed and surrounded my car. I turned to look back, and this bitch was standing on the porch with the money in her hands, counting it. On my daddy and momma graves, if looks could kill she would be dead.

"You're under arrest for the murder of Jory and Matthew Morrison. Anything you say can and will be used against you in the court of law..."

I blanked out because I had just got myself into something I might not be able to get out of. The fact that Im usually smart about things like this pissed me off. If I ever get out of this, she better had moved far away.

When they put me in the car, they drove me to the Cook County Jail. I knew I needed Legend at the moment.

"Can I make a phone call?" I asked the guard. He made me wait for three hours before I was granted a phone call. I was sitting in this cell with no heat, water, and the toilet wasn't working. The room smelled like shit. I threw up three times because of the smell. I called Legend, and he came through like always.

"Just sit tight. I'ma have my lawyer come up and see what's going on." We never talk on the phone, so our conversation was short.

"Thanks, bro."

"Always," he said and hung up.

THE NEXT DAY, I was sitting in front of Legend, Duce, and the lawyer. Legend looked tired, which let me know he was putting in work in the streets.

"We don't need you to say anything," the lawyer said and then handed me some paper and a pen.

I already knew he wanted me to write everything down. It took me about ten minutes, and then I handed him the paper. He didn't even read it. He put it inside his briefcase, and Legend began talking to me.

"Remember when I told you it's time for a change. That's what I meant. These days they don't care about us black men. They want us to destroy ourselves and get us sent away for life. As your brother, I need you to get your shit together. I would hate for something to happen to you. You got three boys that look up to you. Get it together," he said, and I agreed. I don't want my kids to bury me, so I hope I beat this shit and get on with my life.

"Thanks for speaking to my stubborn ass." He laughed, and then we talked a little bit more before they all left.

When I got back to my cell, I noticed some of my things were moved, and some were stolen. Already knowing what was finna go down, I prepared to go down with a fight. The only time this happens was when someone was about to attack you. What they don't know is that I've been a boxer for years.

I turned around, and suddenly two niggas came into my room and tried to attack me, but it was useless. I picked the first one up and threw his ass against the wall. I knew it was painful because he stumbled to get back up. The second one pulled out a knife and tried to cut me, but I grabbed his hand and squeezed it until he couldn't take it anymore.

"AAAHHH, fuck!" I yelled because the other one cut me in my back. It wasn't enough to bring me down, so I made them pay big time.

"You pussy ass niggas," I said and began showing them my skills. When I finished, they both looked like Martin when he got his ass beat.

When the guards came in, they pinned me to the ground. I knew they were going to take me to the hole for thirty days or more. I didn't give a fuck though. I will fight this shit if I have to. As soon as I got inside the room, it was a box with nothing but a pad on the floor, a toilet that was working properly, and some books to read. Since there was nothing else to do, I sat down on the floor and picked a book up, something I haven't done in years.

The first book I opened was called *King and I* penned by Mz. Lady P. The moment I opened it and read the first couple of pages, I knew I wouldn't be able to put it down. This was me, a full week until one of the guards came in and told me I had a family emergency regarding my grandmother. I just held my head down because I had a feeling that no one wanted to feel. When they walked me to the office, I picked up the phone and damn near cried.

"Hello." It was Onari on the phone.

"It's grandma. She was shot and is clinging to life. She was also raped," she said, and I just hung my head down and dropped the phone. No one told me this is the feeling when a loved one is hurt. It felt like I was choking and about to pass out.

"Is everything ok?" the officer asked me. I just shook my head no. No words could be said at this moment. I cried on the floor as soon as I got back to my room because my grandma was special to so many people. Who would want to harm her?

SEVENTEEN
LEGEND

Having to send Onari to Jamaica because of something in Chicago pissed me off. I didn't tell her it was pertaining to that because I know she would think that I'm back on that street shit. Instead, I told her I wanted to plan my birthday in Jamaica with the whole family, and I would join after they all get there.

Days after they made it safely, I tried to find out where the fuck Pike was at. It felt like something was off, but I couldn't put my finger on it, so I called Duce to have a drink.

"Yooo?" he answered while smacking in my ear.

"Damn nigga. Stop chewing like that."

"Fuck you, bro. What's the word?"

"Let's have a couple of drinks. I need to get some shit off my chest."

"Ok, come to my crib."

"Bet," I said and drove straight there.

Once inside, we poured a couple of shots of Henny and began talking shit. We were an hour into drinking when I got a call from Onari on Ms. Rosie's house phone.

I didn't even have to say anything when I answered. She began screaming and hollering, and I couldn't understand what she was saying.

"Take a deep breath. What's wrong?" I stayed calm because I knew whatever she was about to tell me would hurt my heart.

"It's my grandma. She was shot, and blood is all over her face." She was crying so bad, and I felt helpless.

"I'm on my way. Check her pulse."

Duce and I ran out of his house and did ninety on the highway. Now I know what that feeling was earlier. The moment we walked into the crib, my eyes were playing tricks on me. Rosie's clothes were hanging off her, which meant she was raped, and her face was bloody. I checked to see if she was dead, and surprisingly, she wasn't.

"It was Nytrell and Pike. They did this to me." She had cried so much that her face was dried out. I immediately called the doctor we use to keep this shit on the low. We didn't need the police in our business.

"Duce grabbed me a towel to clean her up. Hang on, Ms. Rosie. The doctor will be here shortly."

"I'm ok, son. It's nothing but the Lord keeping me alive." This lady was strong.

"How long have you been here?" I began wiping her face while Duce helped Onari wrap up at the bottom. It took everything in me not to catch a case at this point.

"I don't know," she said and began coughing. I gave her some water when I finished, and some bread because her lips were very dry. She was literally shaking.

"How did you get here?" I kept asking her questions to get to the bottom of this shit.

"I got a call telling me my brother had an asthma attack and he might not make it, so I came back immediately. When I got there, he wasn't even a patient there. That's when I knew something was wrong. I then called an Uber to get me home, and I walked in, and they attack me from behind, and Pike rapped me."

I had to take a deep breath because the things I'm going to do to them will be ten times worse.

"So, Pike raped you, and what did Trell do?"

"He's the one that shot me." Onari was hysterically crying while rocking back and forth. Minutes later, the doctor came in and began working on her.

"Ain't God good," he said while checking the bullet wound.

"The bullet took a small piece of her skull, but she's gone be ok. That is why she is talking. Give me a minute, and she will be good to go."

I told him ok, grabbed Onari, and we walked out to the back porch.

"Why would he do that?" Onari asked me, and I just held her tight. This shit is getting out of hand. I just wanted to get out and live a happy life.

"It's gone be ok. I promise. Just know that after today, y'all will no longer be living here. I'm moving y'all with me, and we gone build from there. I just need you to trust in what im doing."

I didn't even tell her what I had up my sleeve. Shit is about to get real, and when I get done, the whole United States is gone know what happened to them niggas. That's a fact.

"I'm scared."

I felt shitty. My girl was scared to make movements in a city that I'm well known in. I turned her around to me and looked in her eyes. I made sure to wipe her tears and kiss her forehead.

"As long as I'm breathing on this earth, I will let no one, or nothing hurt you. I will kill myself if something happens to you." I held her until she calmed down, and then the doctor walked out about an hour later.

"She is currently sleeping at the moment because I gave her a sleeping pill to keep her from moving the wrong way. I put a little block where the wound was and covered the hole. She will be fine. I also left her some medicine to help it heal faster," he told me, and I handed him some money for helping us.

"Ok. I'ma stay here until she wakes up. Duce, I need you to make that call. We're on everything today."

Once he left, I stayed inside and made sure they were ok. While Rosie was sleeping, Onari and I began packing up clothes and other things because this is the last time they will be here. When Duce called and told me to meet him at Bar 10, I hopped right on it. I couldn't move Ms. Rosie, so I called and had the security surround every inch of the house.

"Here. If you even think something is wrong, you shoot first. I love you, Onari," I told her. I handed her a small gun, and she shook her head.

"I love you too, Legend." I kissed her lips and hopped in my car. Shit was about to get real ugly.

WE SAT and had one drink before Duce's girlfriend Tisha walked in to talk business.

"They're on their way here. Head out to the car," she said and handed me some pictures. Tisha was a private investigator who I hired to make shit simple. I was done playing these cat and mouse games with them. When I found out Nytrell was behind this whole thing, I knew shit was about to get real. In my mind, I don't give a fuck who he is. I just hope Onari can forgive me for killing her brother.

"Thanks, bae." Duce kissed her.

I'm still stuck on how she can deal with his shit. Duce and I became close when we were fucking on the same bitch and didn't know about it. When she got caught up, we both laughed in her face. From that day forward, we'd been homies ever since.

Once we got to the car, they came strolling up the street and didn't even look around them. That's the first mistake. They walked into the bar, realized we weren't in there, and then came out cursing.

"Let those bullets drop," I told Duce, and he did. Being a trained shooter, I taught him how to shoot in the right places.

POW! POW! POW! POW!

He shot both of them in each leg, causing them to drop and scream. Before we pulled off, I made sure that he saw my face. He will wish he never did this shit. Because we knew they wouldn't get far after getting shot, we let them get to this abandoned building and waited outside to make sure no police were following them or us.

ALMOST TWO HOURS LATER, Duce and I walked in on straight business. They both were knocked out, so I immediately picked up a brick and smashed it on top of Pike's head. He couldn't even scream because I hit him so hard. That hit had also knocked most of his teeth out. Blood leaked out causing him to choke.

"Call Troy. We gone need some help with this nigga."

Troy already knew to bring the chains, so Duce and I began tying Trell up. I guess those drugs had him feeling real good because he still didn't budge or move.

Troy came in no time, and we all picked Pike up upside down and chained him hanging from the ceiling.

"Wake that fuck nigga up," I told them while sitting back in a chair smoking a blunt. Shit was about to get real.

"AHHHH!" Trell woke up instantly when Duce grabbed the blowtorch and threatened to burn him. I stopped him though because I wanted to save him for last.

"I want you to sit back and watch what I'ma do to you," I told Trell and stood up. The first thing I did was take the blowtorch and burnt Pike's dick to a crisp.

"This for sticking your dick where it don't belong. Now light his ass up," I told Duce, and he set Pike's ass on fire. When we were finished with him, I focused on Trell.

"I'm not even surprised you had something to do with this. I mean, you are a crackhead, and crackheads do anything to get their next fixed. The fact that you decided to shoot yo grandma when she basically gave you a life to live. Let me not forget to tell you that she is alive and told us everything." His face lit up when I told him that.

"Man, it was all Pike." Trell tried to blame everything on Pike as if I would believe it.

"Shut yo bitch ass up. I don't want to hear shit. Troy, hand me those plyers." I was done talking to him.

"Come on, man. Don't do this." Trell started begging me, and that made me even madder.

When Troy handed me the pliers, they held him while I clipped three of his toes off. I wasn't done though. I then began fucking his skin up with the blowtorch until I thought he would die.

"Man, just kill me."

"I'm just getting started. Hang tight." I laughed because I was gonna make him suffer.

For the next three hours, I did everything you could think of to make him hate me. We had to stuff something in his mouth to keep him from screaming and someone hearing him. When I was done with him, he had several fingers and toes missing, and his whole body was fucked up.

"The next time you ever try to play me or anyone else close to me, it won't be a second chance," I said before leaving him to suffer in pain. With that, we all walked out, and I went back home to stay with Onari. Once Ms. Rosie gets well, we're out of there.

EIGHTEEN

ONARI

When Legend walked into the house, I ran into his arms. I knew whatever he went out to do it wasn't good, so I was worried.

"I just wanna go," I immediately told him, and he nodded his head.

"Everything is already set for us. Once your grandmother gets well we out." It was an awkward moment because he was too quiet. I could tell he was in a deep moment where something was bothering him.

"You ok?" I rubbed his waves to make him relax.

"How would you feel if I asked you to move with me to California? I know it's last minute, but I don't think Chicago got what I'm looking for as far as money and other things. I also want to make sure my whole family is safe. That street shit is not in me no more."

I was shocked because Legend has always been about Chicago. Neither of us has family down there.

"You just want to up and leave?" He grabbed both of my hands and looked deep into my eyes.

"Onari, I already got our house. I've had it since I was in jail. I always knew that when shit in the streets got rough, it's time to move around. I don't have time to sleep with one eye open every night. I also picked the perfect place for you to continue running your business. I don't care if we don't know anybody down there, as long as I got you and you got me, we good. If it makes you feel any better, my family is coming as well. All we need to do is pack and leave."

"What about the things you got going in here? What about your construction license?" I asked him because that's a big step to take.

"I got a couple more hours to go then I'm good. I'ma transfer everything down there and began making my own money. I don't want to work for no one else. I'm tryna become legit."

On the inside, I was happy because I knew things at this point were real. I never imagined myself this deep in love with someone so soon.

"If you're rocking, I'm rolling," he said, and I smiled.

"Good because I'm sick of this cold ass weather."

He finally smiled and kissed my forehead. I just felt like everything would be ok. Once we walked up the stairs to the room, we heard the TV going in my grandma's room.

"Grandma, you're supposed to be sleeping."

"I'm tired of sleeping. Every time I close my eyes, I see those damn demons." I felt bad because I didn't know how bad this would affect her.

"And don't ask me to go see a therapist because I will not. I believe the good Lord will heal my body with no problem." She must have read my mind because I was just about to ask her that. Knowing my grandma, she made up her mind.

"Ok," I said and laid in the bed next to her. I had to be gentle because she was still sore. Legend walked away to give us some privacy, and I watched TV with her until I was sleep.

THE NEXT DAY, I was extremely exhausted from not getting much sleep lately. This was actually the first night I slept well, but I think I slept too long, which is why my body was feeling so tired. When I sat up in the bed, I looked to my left and Legend was just staring at me. It was creepy but sexy.

"Waking up to you is the best feeling in the world," he blurted out and, I smiled while covering my mouth. I hate morning breathe, but he didn't mind.

"The feeling is mutual," I said, getting out the bed to take a shower.

When I finished, I ate some oatmeal so that I could get back to working out. Both Legend and I been slacking when it comes to being healthy.

"Here, it's Nyquan." Legend handed me his phone. I had to get my number changed because Pike was blowing me up almost every day since this stuff happened.

"Hey, brother?" I was excited to hear from him since he was in the hole. When he told me what happened after Legend left, I was pissed. I just wanted all this bad shit to come to an end.

"Hey, wassup, sis?" I could tell he was stressing, but I'm sure Legend gave him some much needed information he could use.

"How's grandma doing?"

"She is doing ok. She is gone live. Now we're focused on moving to California to get away from this crazy place. I don't ever want my daughter to be around this shit."

"Man, when I get out, my boys and me are coming with y'all. Legend finally talked some sense into my thick ass skull." We both laughed, and I brought up the kids and checked in to see how his case was looking.

"Legend handled business like he said, so I should be home in a month or so. My boys are with their godmother until I get out. I just talked to them, and they're good."

I was glad to hear this news. Even though I don't know what Legend went out and did, I do know he is a blessing. When he said he was gone handled it, I think he did just that. We didn't talk about what Trell did because I think we both feel the same about him at this point. Even though my grandma told me to pray for him, I just couldn't. If he's willing to kill the woman who raised him, I could never pray for him. I don't even trust him anymore, and that's from the bottom of my heart.

"I love you, bro. We all we got," I told him before the phone hung up.

"No doubt. Love you too."

When I gave Legend the phone, I tried to walk away, but he pulled me back towards him. I turned around, and he was ass hole naked with that damn dick slanging from left to right. His dick was so pretty and all I wanted to do suck on it. I knew I had to stop being shy around him, so I pushed him on the bed and went to work. I wasn't good at this, but I'ma try my ass off.

"Damn, girl," he immediately said when I wrapped my mouth around the tip, giving it a tight grip. He grabbed ahold of my hair, which turned me on, so I began going down until I couldn't take it any longer. I guess watching porn paid off.

"Ahhh, fuck!" I was looking at him the whole time while he was biting his bottom lip in a sexy way.

When I started feeling his veins getting bigger, I knew he was about to explode, so I pulled away. I stood up, and he helped me pull my leggings and panties down. I don't know where me being so horny came from, but I immediately hopped on top. After a couple of seconds of pain, I was on top riding his dick like a pro.

"Legend, oh my god baby."

"Who pussy is this?"

"Yours, babe, yours." I couldn't even tell him I was cumin'. I let the flood gates open, and so did he. We both exploded, and I collapsed on top of him.

This was us for the next week or so. We fucked in the bathroom, kitchen, and even on my balcony while we were on some drunk shit in the cold. Now I know what it's like to make love and fuck at the same time. I could get used to this.

NINETEEN

NYQUAN

Being home from that hellhole was a blessing. The lawyer Legend got me did exactly what he said he was gone do. When my court date came around, the bitch opened her mouth on accident and said that she and the other two were trying to rob me, and that's when things went bad. He didn't want to hear anything else. He took the charges off me and charged her with their murder. It was that easy.

"You ready to go make yo own bread and stop fucking around in these streets." Legend and Troy came to pick me up with a big ass bottle of D'usse.

"You already know it. Let me change my clothes, go see my kids, and pop out with y'all niggas."

I was beyond happy. Tonight, we were celebrating many things— Legend's birthday since he didn't get a chance to, us leaving for California next week as a family, and me being able to bring my kids thanks to their mom who gave me permission.

"Bro, I appreciate everything you did for me," I told him, and he handed me a rolled up blunt. Us growing up, we never smoked behind each other. We always had our own blunts, so all three of us were smoking until we had nothing left.

"I got you, bro, forever."

Once he dropped Troy off at the car lot he owns, we watched him enter and pulled away. All of a sudden it got quiet, and if anybody knows Legend, you know he was thinking about some shit.

"You know I found out who killed my uncle, right?"

"Who?"

"Trell and Pike. They tried to rob him. I don't even know why I'm surprised." He had been telling me to keep my eyes open around him, but I didn't because we were family."

I could tell this shit was eating him up.

"Let me ask you this. Did you know about this shit?"

I should have known this info wouldn't be buried.

"I didn't know until I went to see Trell in rehab, and he spilled the beans. He told me everything. I didn't say anything because I figured he would get better and eventually tell on himself."

Growing up, niggas don't snitch. We retaliate. This was a no-win situation. We were silent for a minute or so, and then I asked him about Pike and Trell.

"Have you heard anything about them?" I was told they got away, but I know Legend, and he ain't letting that shit slide. Just as he was about to speak, the news came on the radio.

"We are on the scene of a brutal murder on the west side of Chicago. Early this morning, a building inspector walked into one of his properties, and found a body burned, while hanging from the ceiling. There is currently no information on who this person is, or why this happened. Once we get updated information, we will keep everyone posted."

I didn't even need his response, because I knew this was his work. I tried not to think about it being Trell because he was still my brother, but if it is, he brought it on himself.

Once he dropped me off, it didn't take long for me to get dressed. I was so happy that I was literally dancing and rapping in the crib. Before I left out, I grabbed my gun, weed, and my drink. Tonight, about to be lit.

I SHOT to the top just like I'm a rocket(like I'm a rocket), I ain't have a dollar inside my pocket (inside my pocket), put that on my gang, I swear I ain't stopping (I ain't stopping), strapped up and I'm vest up, I'm an astronaut kid. They say pain like meteorites, I got the world in my eyes. The chosen one, I got the prize. I got my niggas on my side.

WALKING INTO DAISIES CLUB, they were playing NBA Young-Boy, and all eyes were on us as usual. Every bitch and nigga from across the globe were in attendance. Whenever Legend's name is mentioned, everybody wants to be a part of it. We don't roll like that though. We got our own section.

"Damn, my nigga. Welcome home, bro." I laughed hard as hell at Duce.

"Nigga, it ain't been that long." We gave each other a brotherly hug. Duce had bitches all around him as usual.

Bottles were being passed around along with weed and pills. Everybody was lit, including Onari and Nastasia who was literally dancing and shaking their ass everywhere. I thought Legend was gone snap, but he didn't. He actually enjoyed the show.

"Damn, daddy. You look real familiar." Some chick walked up to me with a badass body. Her face wasn't too bad looking. I haven't had any sex in a minute, so I was down for some good ass head.

"Oh yea," I said, licking my lips.

I was admiring her shape, and she grabbed me and pulled me to the bathroom. No one was inside, so we locked the door, and she pulled my pants down without a care in the world.

"Damn. Like that." I bit my bottom lip the moment she wrapped her lips around the head of my dick.

She had to be a pro at this shit because she had my dick damn near touching her tonsils with no gag reflexes. Once I started to feel the sensation of me exploding, she used her tongue ring by twirling it around the head, and it was over. I grabbed her hair and let every drop go down her throat.

She stood up and quickly wiped her mouth. I used a paper towel and cleaned her saliva off my dick, and we went back to the party.

"We gone finish this later," I said to her, and she smiled.

"Fosho," she said, and I almost threw up.

Her breath smelled like she had been eating a whole pig. Nothing but the smell of chitterlings was coming out. I didn't even smell her breathe the first time she walked up to me. Now I'm pissed because I made plans to fuck her later. I can deal with a bitch looking half-decent, but when it comes to hygiene bitches gotta come correct. I walked away, and stood by Legend and the guys. They already knew the deal.

"You done fucked stinky breath shawty huh?" Duce said, and they all laughed.

"Naw, she just sucked my dick." I was lowkey embarrassed.

"Good. That bitch got that shit but her throat game crazy." I just held my head down. I should have known this nigga had a piece of her.

ONCE THAT RÉMY started kicking in, I was lit. I was lit to the point that I could barely walk. Around three a.m., the club was getting ready to close, so I staggered to my car. It took me a minute to get inside the car, but I made it. Once I started it, I sat there to gather myself before pulling off.

"I thought we were family," I heard and turned around.

It was Trell sitting in the back seat with a hoodie on his head. The look he was giving me was kind of scary. I also noticed his face was fucked up. I wasn't surprised he broke into my car because he did it before.

"Man gone head on with that shit. The shit you did is something family doesn't do. Get the fuck out my car." I was pissed this nigga had the audacity to say some shit like that. He didn't budge or move. The whole time I was talking, I could hear the sound of something beeping.

"I hope you said goodbye to yo kids." He smirked, and I knew right then and there it was over for me.

BOOOOOOOMMMMMM!

TWENTY

ONARI

Things have been going so good for all of us, and I couldn't have been happier. Since we were moving soon, I transferred all my paperwork to California and made sure everything was set before we get there. I was just ready to live and start all over again. The fact that I have to look over my shoulders everywhere I go is scary.

"Bitch, Legend must don't know you it here cutting up in these streets," Nastasia said when I pulled up to her crib to pick her up. Lately, we've been riding together wherever we went just to be on the safe side. Tonight, we were having a big party at the club for Legend, and for us going away.

"Girl, Legend was just leaving the barbershop, so he told me to go ahead, and he will meet me there. He's gone be surprised," I said, laughing.

Tonight I was rocking a fitted Balmain sweater dress that had my ass sitting right and some Balmain wedge heels to go with it. I had my hair freshly flat ironed and had added a little makeup to complete my look. I know he's gone be going crazy when he sees me. I normally don't dress this way, but tonight I'm on whatever.

As soon as we made it into the club, the line was around the corner. Nastasia and I walked straight to the front, and the bouncer let us right in. He was on Legend's payroll, so I wasn't surprised. He had someone walk us to his section, and it was even worse by the door. Every bitch in Chicago was trying to get inside. Once he cleared them out the way, we walked in, and all eyes were on us.

"I advise you to change before Legend gets here," Duce said when I walked up and hugged him. I knew he already called him because that's how they roll. Plus, he didn't like the stares I was receiving from the other men.

"Shut up," I smirked and then hugged Troy. He too was pissed at Nastasia's clothes. I just pulled her away to the bar.

We both began ordering drinks. I ordered myself a shot of Rémy to get me started, and she laughed.

"I see you, friend. For somebody who really doesn't drink, is ordering above and beyond." Nastasia ordered her a couple of shots along with some Red Bull.

"Ooohh shit. This my song." They began playing that new Cardi B and Bruno Mars song "Please Me". Every girl in there was cutting up. As soon as I bent over, I began twerking my ass off. After too much fun and attention, I slowed down a little and sat back by the bar.

"You got a man?" I heard and smiled hard as hell. The smell of that Ferragamo cologne seeped up my nostrils and made my pussy wet.

I turned around, and Legend was looking real daddyish tonight. With his fresh haircut, Burberry fit from head to toe, along with the shoes, I was ready to jump that dick.

"Yes, I do," I was playing along. He squeezed my ass cheeks and pulled me up for a kiss.

"Not anymore. You mine forever." We continued to kiss until Nastasia stepped in.

"My girl and I are about to go back on the dance floor." She had her hands on her hips.

"That's a no go. She's been shaking her ass all night long. It's my time now."

With Troy right behind her, she knew it was over. When they went their way, Legend and I sat in the chairs to chill. He ordered bottles of champagne and Rémy for everyone in that section.

"How long you been here? You had me waiting."

"I've been here the whole time. I stood in the back and watched you shake yo ass. I almost took you in the back."

He gave me that sexy smirk, and I giggled. I love everything about this man. He gives me fresh butterflies every time I see him.

"Just so we're clear, I don't mind you dancing in the clubs, but never let me hear or see you dancing with another nigga. That shit will get you and him killed. Real shit." The way he said it all calm, but at the same time with a look that said he wasn't playing let me know that he wasn't bullshitting.

I didn't even respond. I changed the subject, dancing and grinding all over him. He sat back and enjoyed the show while throwing money all over my ass. I could see the looks of other bitches balling their faces up. I'm glad I snatched him up because that would probably have been me.

Once I got all into it, I spotted my brother who I didn't even know came. I guess he was entertaining the stinky breath girl everyone was talking about. When I saw him stumble, I stopped and told Legend to make sure he ok. I know how Quan gets when he is lit. He be ready to fight everyone. He got up and went to check on him.

"He's good. I told him no more drinks." He sat back down and whispered sweet nothings in my ear, making me blush.

"I'm ready for a baby. You ready?"

"You want me to answer that?" I asked him knowing that I was all for it. The way he treats my daughter is rare. He had literally walked into my daughter's life out of nowhere and became her dad. She called him dada, and he responds with passion. I love it.

"No, you don't. I believe you already pregnant."

"How you figured that?"

"Because you haven't bought any tampons in almost a month and a half." I laughed hard as hell because he wasn't lying. The fact that he knew this kind of scared me.

"So, you watching my every move?"

"You damn right. That's my pussy, and I got to know everything." We laughed and joked until it was time to leave.

Once I stood up, I was a little drunk, but not to the point that I didn't know what was going on.

"Where's Quan?" I asked Duce who was cuddled up with his girl.

"He was in the bathroom the last time I checked. Let me go see. Bae, get valet to bring the car," he told her and walked to the car.

I think Legend sensed something was wrong and told me don't move. I couldn't sit still though. I went over to Nastasia and told her to help me find Quan. We immediately walked towards the front entrance and stepped outside. When I spotted him sitting in his car but turned like he was talking to someone, it let me know he was ok. I breathed a sigh of relief and started walking to his car to make sure he was ok.

I wasn't even halfway to the car when I heard a loud explosion. The only thing I remembered was my ears ringing like crazy. Anything after that was a blur.

———————

TWO DAYS LATER, I woke up in a lot of pain. The pain was coming from different spots on my body. When I looked over at Legend holding my right hand, and my grandma holding the left hand praying, I knew something bad happened. For her to be out of bed this soon let me know something was wrong.

"What happened?" I immediately asked in a scratchy voice.

"It was Quan and Trell. They were in an explosion inside Quan's car. They both died, but you and Nastasia survived," my grandma said, and I was confused.

"We didn't get in the car with them?" I'm still tryna figure out where the fuck Trell came from. We haven't seen or heard from him since all that stuff went down.

"You were walking to Quan's car when the car blew up." I swallowed the lump in my throat. Looking down at my hands let me know that I was burned.

"Hand me a mirror," I told Legend who was quiet the whole time.

He handed me the mirror and put his head down. Half of my head was wrapped, and my cheek was burned as well. I literally bawled my eyes out. This is not happening to me right now.

TWENTY-ONE

LEGEND

I knew shit wasn't good when Duce came out of the bathroom and told me Quan was not in there, so I immediately got on top of it. I was just talking to him and told him no more drinking. He was fucked up.

"Shut this bitch down. Don't let anyone in or out," I said, pulling my gun out and Duce followed.

Troy was still walking around the club asking females have they seen him. Just when I was about to blast any nigga that looked like they had something to do with him being missing, we heard a big ass explosion. That shit was so close that it had my fucking ears ringing. Everyone began to run outside, stepping on other people and knocking them down to get out. The first thing I saw when I stepped outside was Quan's car on fire. I knew it was over for him because you could see his body burning in the front seat.

"Nastasia!" Troy yelled, and we all ran to her. She was on the ground in a daze. Other people who were out there when it happened was hurt as well.

"Where is Onari?" I said, looking around for her and calling her name. I started to panic hoping that she wasn't in the car with Quan.

"Someone help her!" some female yelled, and I noticed that it was Onari on the ground. She was a few feet from the club but behind some bushes.

I ran to her and almost went crazy. She was burned badly, and some parts of her face, hands, and legs were fucked up.

"Everybody step the fuck back." Duce and some of my other homies were keeping people away from her. Troy was still by Nastasia's side.

"I'm so sorry, baby," I said while trying to wrap her body with my shirt that I took off. I knew she was alive because she was breathing really slowly.

When the police and ambulance came, they grabbed Onari and Nastasia and took them to the hospital. The police were trying to get information from everybody while they waited on the coroner to arrive. I was gone investigate this shit myself, so we played dumb, and after that, I went to the hospital.

Once we got there, I called my mom to come up there, but to my surprise, Ms. Rosie came instead. I didn't call her because she was already going through a lot. She was also still healing.

"Your mom called me, and I didn't take no for an answer. I figured she should stay with Aniyah and Lil' Troy and let us figure this out. Where is my granddaughter?"

I didn't question shit because I knew she made up her mind. I couldn't even tell her what happened. I was in a daze just walking back and forth waiting on the results.

"Onari's gone be ok, ma. She and Nastasia were near Quan's car when it blew up," Troy came out and said, trying not to sound harsh. I knew he was fucked up in the head as well.

"Where is Quan?" No one responded so she knew he didn't survive. I thought she was going to spazz, but she didn't. She held her head up, and that's when I got up to hug her.

HOURS AFTER WAITING, the doctor walked out with good news.

"Nastasia is going to be ok. She had minor bruises along with some deep cuts that we closed. She is good to go. As for Onari, she had to get some of her skin removed from her left leg and apply it to her face. She has other burns that we covered and is being treated. She lost a small amount of her hair on the side, but she will be ok.

Right now, she will be here until were finish grafting her skin and making sure she heals properly. The good thing is that we didn't have to go deep to get skin." He handed us some papers to sign.

"Can we go in and see her?"

"Only one for now because she needs to get some rest. Everyone else will have to wait until tomorrow." I told him ok and asked Ms. Rosie if she wanted to go.

"No, go ahead. I will see her tomorrow. I need to call and give the news to his boys. They don't know anything."

"Ok, handle that and keep me posted."

I then walked into the room, and Onari was wrapped up tightly. I couldn't see her head, but I did notice some parts of her skin were gone. It looked like they applied some cream on the minor cuts. I just sat down, grabbed her hand, and said a small prayer. My uncle always told me a praying man is a powerful man. I might not have attended church, but I believe in the good Lord himself, and I have faith in everything he does.

"Lord, all I ask is for you to heal my baby so that we can live our life. I know I was messed up in the past, but I'ma changed man. Please heal her. Please."

I didn't realize I had tears coming down my cheek until I rubbed my eyes. Just seeing her like this fucked me up. I sat in the room with her for thirty minutes before I had to leave.

"She's gone be ok," Rosie said to me when I walked out. We kept trying to keep each other uplifted. Her grandma was one strong lady. She had been through a lot when it comes to death and still managed to go on with her life day by day.

Once Troy and Nastasia went home that night, Ms. Rosie and I stayed with Onari. I had Duce go and get us some changing clothes and some personal items. I didn't want her to wake up, and I'm not there.

THE NEXT MORNING, I took a quick shower and was about to go down to get Ms. Rosie and me some breakfast, but some detectives walked in the room. We already knew Quan was dead from the scene, so I didn't understand why they were there. We don't know shit.

"Hi, Ms. Williams. I'm Detective Tinoco?" The detective gave her a handshake when she walked into the room.

"Call me Ms. Rosie," she said with a sad face.

"Ok, Rosie. We were already informed that you were aware of Quan's death. We've been investigating his tragic accident and found out there was another person in the car with him. When we got dental records, and the results came back to a Nytrell Williams, which we assumed is his brother."

I literally fell out of the chair when she said that. All I wanted to know now was this shit intentional.

"Are you serious?" Rosie asked.

"Yes, ma'am. The corner confirmed both of their deaths. The fire crew investigated as well and found some type of explosive near Nytrell's body. They confirmed that he let the explosive go off and killed both of them. We don't know why, but if you have any questions regarding their deaths, please give me a call."

She handed her a card, hugged her, and walked out. Now we gotta bury both of them. Shit is getting worse.

"Whatever the cost is, just let me know so that I can take care of everything," I told Ms. Rosie. She had already called the funeral home for the memorial of Quan, but now we gotta call for Trell as well.

"Thanks so much. I really appreciate everything you've been doing for us. I done been through a lot these last couple of weeks, but the way you keep me uplifted is everything," she said, hugging me.

"Don't thank me. I just want to make sure you and everyone else is ok. I failed when I couldn't protect you from the demons, but from this day forward, I got you." She smiled and that's when teardrops fell from her eyes.

"If you don't mind, can you, Troy, and Duce make the funeral arrangements? My mind is not ready for the truth."

"I got you."

She stayed behind, and we all linked at the funeral home to set everything up. Even though Nyquan and Trell will not be viewable, we still gotta go hard for them. Once we got there, I asked for my girl Malisha who's in charge of Grace and Mercy Funeral Services in Chicago. She is one of the best funeral directors out right now.

"Tell me how much you're trying to spend?" We were sitting at the table while she began writing things down.

"No budget."

"Everything you need is in this book. From caskets to flowers and anything else needed to bury a loved one. I already know the condition of both bodies, so I figured you would be cremating them."

"We really don't have a choice. I still wanna go all out."

"Ok, no problem. We can rent some caskets, and we go from there."

"Ok." when she left the room, we already knew what we wanted.

"We should put that bitch ass nigga in a cardboard box," Duce said, not wanting to put Trell in a Promethean casket.

"I'm only doing it because of Rosie and Onari. If it was another nigga, they ass could float down the river for all I care. I just wanna get this over with and be on my way with my family. Chicago ain't like it used to be. Niggas hate instead of jumping on the money team. When we bury them, I'm out," I said, wrapping it up with him. When Duce gets pissed, he doesn't let shit go. I didn't mind spending the money on the caskets because they were being rented anyway, and we didn't have to put down too much.

"Are you ready?" Malisha came back in and asked us.

It took us a couple of minutes to finalize everything, and then we signed some papers. I paid for everything with the funeral home, and Duce and Troy paid the money to have them cremated after.

"I'ma hit y'all up later. I need to get back to Onari," I told them and got inside my car.

TWENTY-TWO
ONARI

Waking up to this type of news fucked me up. Not only did both my brothers die, but my face, hands, and legs are fucked up in certain places. After crying my eyes out for almost ten minutes, my grandma and Legend tried to comfort me the best they could.

"We're gone be alright. In order for me to be strong, I need you to be strong as well. We're gone get through this together."

"I know, but why did this have to happen to me, to us, to our family? Now, I look like a fucking monster. Look at my face."

"God closes doors to open up new ones. We never know what he is planning on doing, but overall, we have to trust in him and trust that he will bring the best out of any situation. Aniyah needs you, and so does that unborn baby you're carrying."

I quickly wiped my eyes when she said that.

"What you mean?"

"The doctors ran some tests and told us you were four months pregnant. Thank God the baby is ok," she came out of nowhere and said. I then looked over at Legend who was calm as if he was saying I told you so. I shouldn't even be surprised because we never used a condom.

It was all too much at one time. I tried to sit up, but the pain throughout my body was unbearable.

"The doctors don't want you to make no movements at this moment. He wants you to rest up some more before your skin grafting again." I didn't even reply. I just turned my body away from them and silently cried. I felt like shit.

A COUPLE OF HOURS LATER, I woke up to Legend trying to get me to eat.

"I'm not hungry. I just want to sleep."

"Naw, fuck that. We are not about to play when it comes to my unborn baby. Get up, ma. You need to eat. Fuck the bullshit." I had to turn slowly to face him. He just snapped out of nowhere.

"Look, we're all fucked up about this, but drowning in yo tears is not gone help shit. I lost one of the realest niggas I knew. Quan wasn't just yo brother. He was my brother as well. It's hurting me too."

"Look at me, Legend. My face and body are fucked up, all because of you and the streets!" I yelled at him and regretted saying it.

"Fuck you mean me and the streets? When I got out, I was on nothing but positive shit. The moment they gave me all those years, I gave it all up. Name one wrong thing I did when I got out? The only thing I did wrong was help Trell out, and it backfired. The only wrong I did was not protect you and your grandma from those niggas. Don't blame shit else on me."

This was the first time he exploded on me.

"You're right. I'm sorry. I don't know what to do at this point. Like everything was going so good for me." I was all out of tears. I just closed my eyes to breathe slowly. I suddenly felt him grab my hands and hold them to his heart.

"Onari, you know me from way back in the days. I'm talking about high school days. I have never been the type to show emotions until you let me in. This shit right here let me know how I can't survive without you by my side. I don't give a fuck about my past. All I know is that we are the future. This shit is a process, but we're gone heal together. I don't care if it takes years, but we're gone get through it."

"I know." I opened my eyes, and the look in his eyes gave me confidence that everything gone be ok.

"These scars are small shit to a giant." He picked the mirror back up so that I can see myself.

"As long as you know that I love you for what's inside and not the outside, that's all that matters. Beauty scars are what we gone call them. I got you, ma. I love you, girl." He kissed the back of my hand and rubbed my face.

"I love you too."

"Now eat this food before I beat yo ass for playing with my baby. She's hungry." I laughed because he was overdoing it now. He always found a way to make any situation better.

"You mean he?"

"Naw she. I don't wanna raise no boys. I want to raise a young princess into a queen."

"Whatever. I just want my boy, and then I will be set— one girl and one boy." He helped me sit up so that I could eat. Some of the pain was gone because of the pain meds.

"Now you cappin'. We gone start slow then ease into a team of vicious girls, savages."

"Legend, you got life fucked up." He laughed, but I know he was serious.

We talked all day long, and I was able to see my daughter and Nastasia. I was glad that she was ok.

"You don't want to go home and get some rest?"

"Naw, I'ma rest when we get you out of here. Right now, I don't want you to worry about me." He was sleeping in the chair that let all the way back. He turned the TV on, and we watched a couple of movies before I went to sleep.

TWO WEEKS LATER, I was able to be released from the hospital early to attend my brothers' memorial. Legend didn't want them to cause more pain on my body, so we all agreed to leave some of the scars as is. It's been a lot going on, but they waited until I was able to move around on my own.

"How are you feeling?" Nastasia asked me while she was helping me get ready. I was glad she was around to keep me sane.

"I'ma be ok. It just feels weird that I no longer have my brothers. It's hard. I don't care what Trell did. He was still my brother, and no amount of anger will ever make me hate him. I just have to except he was battling a disease that took over his life," I told her with a slight smile.

My heart was beating fast because I wasn't ready to let go of them just yet.

"Y'all ready?"

Legend walked into the room in an all-black Givenchy suit from head to toe. He and all the guys were in black, and us women and children were in white Givenchy outfits. I wasn't comfortable with a dress, so I wore some fitted leggings with a white blouse. Quan's three boys were in gold. I felt bad as fuck for my nephews. Those boys had been taking it hard. I have to thank Legend, Troy, and Duce for stepping up and helping them through this. I know they will be ok.

"Yea, unfortunately." He walked over, grabbed my hands, and walked me down the stairs. The Maybach was outside waiting for Nastasia and me.

"Let's get this over with." Once I stepped outside, the rain and chill didn't make it any better. It felt so gloomy that I couldn't do shit but cry.

"We're gone celebrate their lives and move on. I don't want no tears inside, so get them all out now."

My grandma was tired and wanted everything to be over with like me. She gave me the eye because I knew she was talking about me. Plus, I'd been stressing since I found out I was pregnant. The constant throwing up and peeing is ridiculous.

Once we got to the funeral home, Legend held my grandma and my hands until it was over. He made sure we didn't break. The comfort from everyone was what we needed, including his sons. All three of them held their emotions and hung their heads high. I know Nyquan taught them well. After the last couple of funny remarks about Quan, my grandma shut it down.

Since they were both being cremated, we all drove to the club where they both were killed, and let some balloons go. I didn't even want to get out of the car because I kept hearing the sound of the explosion. I was constantly telling myself that I should have paid more attention to him in the club. Maybe we wouldn't be here right now.

"Here." Legend handed me a bottle of water and rubbed my forehead.

"You good?"

"I'ma be ok. I'ma stay here with Nastasia," I told him, and he walked off to where everyone else was standing.

"Dada." Aniyah began crying for him as soon as he walked off. He got her so spoiled that I don't know what to do sometimes.

"I would have never thought Legend would be a dad. He has always been soft on kids, but the main things were if he didn't plan to spend the rest of his life with one woman, then there was no need for kids. A two-parent household is everything to him since we only had my uncle and mom. I know he gone do right by you and Aniyah," Nastasia said, playing with her.

"Remember when I first met Pike? My dad was bragging and introducing him to everyone that he was gone be my man. I knew he just wanted someone to take care of me if something ever happened my dad. To get that call that he and my mom were killed in a hit and run accident fucked me up. I just needed that support continuously from Pike, but I didn't get it. I didn't understand the things that were happening until I found out that he was in it for money. He knew my parents had money, and he preyed on me to get close to it."

"How did you find out?"

"My grandma just received some papers on a policy that was never cashed in. A policy we knew nothing about. My dad opened an account where if he died, the money inside was for us. Apparently, Pike forged his signature on some recent documents changing names so only he could receive the money. This was right before he was killed. It's all a mess. The good thing is he never got to touch any of it, and now my family and me sitting on millions of dollars."

"Do you ever think of Pike and how things could have turned out?" I knew she was referring to the things I heard Legend did to him. I tried not to think about what happened, and focus on my babies and me.

"I don't think about him at all. The things they did to my grandma fucked me up. However, I don't agree with the way they killed him, but it's all over now. I don't have to deal with him or anyone else. I don't have to look over my shoulders anymore and wonder if he's going to harm me next."

"Enough of him, let's start the healing process." She hugged me, and once it was all over, we all went out to eat instead of a repast. Legend and the guys kept shit simple. California was our next move. I was ready and didn't plan to look back.

"I love you, girl," he whispered in my ear while rubbing my tiny baby bump. I didn't notice it until they told me. I always had a small pudge, but when it starts forming, I knew it was the real deal. We were cuddled in the bed while watching the little light spark through the window. This gave me hope that the future for us would be everything my dad ever wanted.

"Love you too."

TWENTY-THREE

LEGEND

It's been three months since we made the big move to California. The house that I already had down here, I applied a little more work to it with the help of Troy and Duce. It turned out perfect for our little family that's growing. Duce and his girlfriend Tisha, Troy and my sister, and my mom got their own cribs down the block. We all wanted to stay close, but now I regret it because my mom never goes home now. Most of all, my beautiful queen Onari's skin had healed where the burn spots were. The only issue we're having is her dealing with the looks of others when we go out.

The doctors wanted to do a skin graft, but I wasn't feeling that. She was now seven months pregnant and will be due in two months if not before, so we don't need no fuck ups. As long as her family and I were ok with how she looks, that other shit doesn't matter. She is still my little porcelain doll. From time to time, I catch her trying to apply makeup, but I quickly shut that shit down.

"Ma, what do you want?" I said as soon as I walked inside from the heat.

I was outside building a playground for the kids, which was

coming along well. I was sweating bullets going in and out the heat. I forgot how hot California could get.

"This is Onari's shit, bitch." She came out of nowhere on that tough shit.

Growing up, my momma gave us tough love. She gave us tough love because she never us to be weak. If we cried, we were all types of bitches until we got heart. I just got used to her and her ways.

"Says who?"

"Says me," Onari jumped in to defend her like always. They gang up on me every chance they get. That's what I get for spoiling them. I give them whatever they want with no questions asked.

"Whatever," I said and sat down to rest a little.

All I been doing was making major moves and never sleeping. My main goal was to keep pushing. Even my lawyer gave me good news saying the judge is cutting some of my parole time because of what I've been doing. The only issue I'm facing is if they find out that I'm in California. I'm not supposed to leave Chicago until I am fully off of parole.

"Here, babe." Onari walked in front of me and gave me a cold glass of water and my plate of food that she cooked.

She was looking real edible at the moment. If my mom weren't here, I would have bent her over right at that moment. Since she's been pregnant, her weight went all in her ass while her stomach looks super small. She didn't look like most pregnant woman.

"Thanks, ma." She leaned down to kiss me, and I grabbed her ass cheeks.

She's been holding shit down like a wife, and I ain't even asked her to marry me yet. I don't have to worry about anything because the shit is gone already be set and ready for me.

"Onari, baby, what it do?"

I looked up and my cousin who we call Solo popped up like always. Had I known he was down here, I would have picked another city. He was the definition of petty, irritating, and everything above.

The only good thing I can say was he had his own money and was doing a lot of modeling gigs in Cali.

"Hey, boo." They hugged each other, and Solo sat down to gossip.

"So bitch, are you still gone pop out tonight?" I frowned because he know Onari is pregnant, and he constantly asking if she gone pop out. With the look I gave her, she knew how to answer the question.

"Naw, wait to I drop this load. It's crackin' then."

"That shit is so dead." He and Nastasia were trying to turn her out, and I wasn't having it. She rolled her eyes as if I gave a fuck.

"Stop stressing her out."

"Go home, ma."

"Give me some money, and I'm gone."

I just shook my head because she was over petty. I handed her some dollars, and she walked out. Once Solo left, I broke shit down to her.

"We moved down here to get away from the bullshit. Solo is cool, but I'm not feeling how close he's tryna be with you."

"Legend, are you serious? Solo is gay. He doesn't like pussy." She laughed, but I wasn't laughing.

"Yes, the fuck I am," I said, finishing my food while she talked shit to me.

When she finished, I washed the dishes even though she hated when I did that. Most women these days don't go by the old rule where women cooked, cleaned, and washed while the man worked. I don't really care about all of that as long as we eat as a family. I'm the nigga that wants his lady to get out and make their own bread.

"You ready before I go out with the guys?" I asked her because every day we walk to exercise until she has the baby. She be tired, but I don't want her to be the girl that gets lazy when she drops that load. Plus, it was nice as hell outside.

"Yea, let me slip my sandals on and grab Aniyah and Lady." Lady was the new dog that we got for Aniyah. It was a small Yorkie, and Aniyah was crazy about it.

"Dada. Dog," Aniyah said in her baby talk tryna pick it up. She was too advanced for her age.

"Mama, he's too big for you," I said, laughing.

When she began to cry, I let her hold the leash until we got to the park. Right before we got there, I spotted this homeless dude who always gave Aniyah a toy whenever we came here. He looked sick today.

"You ok, my mans?" I asked while walking towards him.

"I'm hungry." He had a cup begging for food, but no one was willing to give him a dime. They probably figured that he would smoke it up.

"Here."

I handed him the tank top off my back, my shoes I was wearing and gave him a twenty-dollar bill. I don't know the feeling of being homeless, but I always help the homeless out. Who knows, that twenty might take him far.

"Thanks, man."

"It's all good." He got up and shook my hand. I called for my mom to bring me an extra pair of shoes while we sat on the bench to let Aniyah play.

"You have a good heart, bae. That's why your blessings keeps pouring in." She grabbed my hand and squeezed it.

"I try when I can."

"I love you so much and happy to say you're my man." That shit made a nigga blush.

"I love you too, ma. Now hurry up and drop that load so that I can bend you all the way over to your toes." I had to throw that in there. Since she's been pregnant, I can't toss her around like I want to, but when she drops, it's over with.

"Ok, Zaddy." She giggled, and I pulled her close to kiss her lips.

We laughed and cracked joke after joke until the sun began to come down. We lived near many trees with little streetlights, so we headed home a little early. Once we got back in the crib, I made sure that they were straight before I walked out. Duce was having a gambling night at his crib, so I was down for some fun.

"Look at this house nigga. He's been hiding like a motherfucka." Troy said while pouring him some Rémy.

"Nigga, you cappin'. My sister got yo ass pussy whipped, so you're in the same boat."

Everybody laughed because he knew it was the truth. Almost every nigga in here had a girl at home that was wifey and didn't bullshit around. The only difference was, most of them cheat and never get caught.

"Pull a chair up and help me get this money, nigga."

"Say no more."

Duce had every table in the house going from deuces, spades, bingo, and other card games. He even had a couple of dice games going. Playing a game of Deuces with them was like a fight. Each hand was twenty dollars, and we do extra side bets.

"I don't want to hear shit when I walk away with everything," Duce said while talking shit before the game started. I sat down, and we began to play.

HOURS INTO US PLAYING, I realized it was going on two in the morning, and more people had come. It turned into a party and bitches was lined up as well.

"Here hold my seat while I check on my girl," I said and gave someone else my seat. As soon as I got up, I bumped into a bitch I used to fuck with years ago when I came down here.

"Wassup, Legend. You don't know a bitch now that you moved down here with yo girl?" She was flirting, but I wasn't on that. I moved here for a better life with my family. I'm not fucking it up for a thot ass bitch.

"Wassup, Samantha. I ain't on shit."

I tried to go around her to keep the confusion down. I don't need no one telling shit on me, especially my sister because she walked right in on good bullshit with Troy.

"Damn, it's like that? We need to link one day."

Before I could respond, Nastasia jumped in front of us on some rah-rah ass shit.

"Does Onari know you still out?"

"Mind ya business." I went around her because she had me fucked up. I tried to call Onari, but she wasn't answering, so I decided to leave.

"I'm gone y'all," I said and noticed that Duce was shacked up with some bitch in the corner. I knew he would be fucking her tonight because his hands were all inside her pants.

Walking to my car, all I could hear was windows busting. I looked and Duce's girl Tisha was holding a bat like a crazy woman. I shook my head, called his ass, and got in my car. Not my problem. I slowly pulled away laughing until I made it to my crib.

For some reason, I was thirsty to lay up under Onari as if I haven't seen her in years. Walking into the room and seeing her underneath the covers made me smile. I wish I would fuck it up for a bitch with no future plans. I got completely naked, climbed in the bed with her, and opened her legs as far as they would go. I woke her up with the power of my tongue, and from there, we fucked all night long.

TWENTY-FOUR

DUCE (DONTE ACTKINS)

"That D'usse makes niggas get loose. Yo dumb ass should have never let the bitch come. I told yo ass don't do it." Troy was helping me clean all the glass from the inside of my car after Tisha bust my windows. I was mad as hell.

"When I catch her I'm breaking her fucking jaw. She got me fucked up."

I had to close the crib down because she ruined it and was about to fight some hoes that she didn't even know. I didn't think she would pop up, but I guess I was wrong.

Tisha and I been fucking around for years, but it never got serious. She was always on the go when it came to her job as a private investigator. That worked perfectly for me because I didn't have to commit. I'm not a committing type of nigga anyway. I like my freedom, but somehow she forgot what this really was. I'm a nigga that's gone keep it one hundred. She knew this shit from the beginning. I fucked with her hard, but shit like this I don't do.

"Man, leave that shit alone. Go home and get some rest. You falling off, nigga. I told you don't let the bitch come over because she's an opp and we don't know her like that. Then all of a sudden all of her friends pop up. Pussy got you tripping."

I couldn't disagree. All the shit we went through in Chicago should have woke me up.

"You right, bro."

When we finished, I pulled my car in the garage and locked it up. Once I knew he and Nastasia made it home, I jumped in the shower to get this liquor smell off me. As soon as I walked out of the bathroom, Tisha was sitting on the bed looking like a crazy woman with a gun on her lap.

"So, you wanna keep playing with me?" I swear I thought she was finna bust a cap in my ass. I had to back the fuck up. My dick was slanging everywhere, but I didn't give a fuck.

"Girl, you crazy for real. Put that gun up before you make a mis..." I couldn't even finish my sentence. She raised it, shot one time, and it went over my head.

"Tisha, come on man." I tried to jump in the closet, but when I felt the bullet rip through my ass cheek, I wanted to die. That shit was painful.

"Aaahhh! You bitch."

"You got me fucked up. I could have stayed in Chicago for this shit. You a disrespectful bastard, and I fucking hate yo ass. Now let's see if the bitch gone fuck with you now. Yo booty all fucked up," she said and walked away. Tisha and I always fought, but this time she was taking shit to the next level.

"Don't fucking leave me, man. I need help!" I yelled because blood was leaking out like a motherfucka. She kept going while I tried to get to my phone to call somebody. Just when I crawled to the bed, my phone began to ring.

"Grandma, she shot me." I was about to cry like a bitch because that wasn't no regular gun she shot me with.

"That's what the fuck you get. Me and yo granddaddy are on the way. Do you want me to call the police?"

"Naw because she gone lose her job and go to jail. Just call the doctor and hurry so that I can get this bitch out my ass."

"Ok, here we come." I've been shot plenty of times, but this one is no joke. I laid there for almost ten minutes, and then I heard them come in.

"Ass shot, huh? You a dumb ass. She should have shot you in yo dick. Keep that motherfucka put up and you won't have this problem. You fucking up my pussy plans." My granddaddy went ham on my ass. He was a lowkey player, which is where I got it from.

"Pussy plans with who?" My grandma pulled her box cutter out.

"Ok, I'ma need y'all to step out while I handle this," the doctor said. I'm sure he used to seeing this shit when it came to my family. We argue and fight all day long, but don't fuck with us because it can be deadly.

"Lay on your stomach," Doc told me while putting towels all around me. He had all his equipment ready to get this bitch out. He gave me a shot in my ass to numb it, and then minutes later, I was out of it.

"GET YO ASS UP, STUPID ASS." I slowly opened my eyes, and Legend was standing there smoking a blunt.

"What time it is?" I could see the sun coming through the window. Then I looked to the left of me while still being on my stomach, and noticed Tisha leaning against the wall.

"It's going on twelve. That ass shot knocked you the fuck out. Let me help you up." He helped me get up while I kept my eye on her ass.

"Tisha, what the fuck man? You already shot me, so now what?" One tear fell from her eye, and she pulled out the spare key that I gave her for emergencies.

"I moved down here hoping that we could change the way this relationship was going and be a family. That's what you told me. You told me that and a lot of other bullshit. We were supposed to be living together, but somehow, you felt it was better to be in our own space. The fact that you are entertaining bitches out in the open lets me know the respect you have for me. From this day forward, you don't have to worry about me. Here are your keys to the cars and the house. Goodbye, Donte." She wiped that tear and walked away.

"You know you fucked up, right? All this time I thought y'all were living together. You foul, nigga."

"Fuck her." I was pissed, but it is what it is. Once I stood up, I took a shot of Rémy to numb the pain because I had to get to the money.

"Nigga, what the fuck you doing? Get some rest. Troy and I got this."

We were currently working on this big ass mansion, and I didn't want to take no chances of fucking my man's money up. Once Legend's license came back, he put it to use. Every call he got, he jumped on it. I was happy to help him out in any way that I could.

"Naw, G. We gotta keep the money flowing."

"It's gone flow now sit yo ass down." Legend helped me down to the living room and laid the pillow on the couch.

"Y'all look like two fuckin' faggots. You act like you his bitch the way you caring for him." Granddaddy June was starting his bullshit early as hell.

"Fuck you, nigga," Legend told him while laughing. Since we've been down here, Legend had gotten very close to my granddaddy. I knew it was him missing his uncle.

"Now how you gone wipe yo ass. If you even look this way, I'ma bust you right in yo shit."

"I'm not handicap. I can still wipe with yo old wrinkled ass." My granddad and I were close as well, so close that we talk shit to each other then the next be watching a basketball game together.

"Suck my dick, bitch!" he yelled, and I couldn't do shit but shake my head.

THE NEXT COUPLE OF DAYS, I started to feel the pain slowly leaving because my peoples wouldn't let me be great. I couldn't do too much because I could possibly rip my stitches. The only problem I run into is when my grandparents leave for the night. I figured they were tired of coming back and forth, so now they come every morning to make sure I'm good. Even though they live about two miles away, I know they have other things to do. I found myself about to call Tisha, but reality set in that she was the reason I was in this situation. Now, this shit is hitting me because I really need her.

"Aye, bitch, get the fuck up," Solo said, coming through the patio door with Troy and Legend.

"Man, fuck this shit."

I was lowkey pissed that I couldn't make moves right now. I slowly sat up on the couch so I can get up and walk. Money was calling, and so was my hoes. Being out of commission was fucking me up.

"Come on the patio so that we can chop shit up on this project coming up," Legend said, grabbing beers out the fridge.

"What the fuck Solo got to do with this?" I'm not gone front, I don't do well with gay niggas, but Solo is a get money nigga. I guess since he was Legend's cousin he gets a pass.

"Just know the more brains on this operation, the more money that's gone come through," he said, walking out to the patio. Once I got out there, I sat a soft pillow in the chair and sat down.

"That shit looked like it hurt." Troy slid me a beer.

"It did. She fucked me up, man."

"You fucked yourself up. I told you not to trust these hoes when we came up here. It was all fun and games when we were visiting and didn't have families and responsibilities. You can't let that shit get in the way," Legend tried to break it down.

"Before I moved down here, Tisha knew how shit would play out."

"Bro, I'm confused. One minute Tisha's yo soon to be wife, then the next you say she's yo bitch like she doesn't mean shit to you. I could never," Troy threw his two cents in.

"What do you want? Man to man." Legend flamed his blunt up and leaned back in his chair.

"I honestly don't know. I like the fast life, but at the same time, moments like this when I need her, it hits me hard."

These niggas were looking at me like I was a fool.

"Ok, look. We done had some of the baddest bitches from the Bahamas all the way to Jamaica. We even had bitches who couldn't speak English make their way to Chicago. It was all fun, but after that, they don't mean shit. How many days can you go without Tisha or even thinking about what she's doing?"

"Shit, barely a day. I'm going crazy right now." I was being honest.

"Exactly. Them other hoes don't mean shit, bro. If you want a life with the bitches, then let Tisha walk away. If you want Tisha and only her, the bitches gotta go. You ain't missing shit. Pussy comes in different shapes and sizes. That's it," Legend laid it on me thick.

"You know what in seeing? I see you being greedy. You want Tisha, but you want everyone else too. I'm sure you and Tisha had this friend agreement thing when y'all first started talking, right?"

"Yep," I replied to Solo. He swore he knew everything about relationships.

"That was then. Now, Tisha wants more, and you don't. That's fine, but like Legend said, you have to let her completely go her way. Not halfway, but all the way. Tisha is a different type of female. She can love you today and hate you tomorrow. That ass shot is a prime example." They all fell out laughing.

"Fuck y'all. What are we talking with this project?" I changed the subject because they were pissing me off with this love shit.

"Ok. Right now, we're doing ok. We got a big ass offer from the housing authority here in Cali. I'm talking about bands, bro. They want us to remodel the apartments and bring them to life. Solo came in because he already had something going with the young girls over there. If it weren't for him, this probably wouldn't be happening. He's into modeling, so why not put it all together and make more money. If they are willing to pay, why not deliver and deliver very well."

I sat back when Legend finished and thought long and hard.

I'm used to fast and illegal money. Since he's been out, he hasn't turned down an offer when it comes to making money. As long as his family eats, everything should be ok.

"I'm down. Now, where do I fit in." I rubbed my hands together.

"Since you're down at the moment, I' ma send you pictures, and you bring it to life with your vision. It's go hard or go home time."

I might have been street all my life, but when a motherfucka put a blank piece of paper in my face, nothing is safe. Art was my favorite subject, and I delivered every time. I just wish I could have pursued my dreams instead of fucking around in the streets.

"Bet money, bro. That don't mean I'm about to be a sucka ass house daddy like you. You went from being the man to being the boy," I blurted out, pointing to Legend.

"He's gone be crying tomorrow when Tisha find a new nigga," Troy threw in there on some hating shit because Nastasia and Onari had them pussy whipped.

"Fuck all y'all." For the rest of the evening, they got drunk with me until their curfew hit, and the girls were calling for them.

TWENTY-FIVE
ONARI

Waking up every morning not knowing how my day will go is stressful. Ever since the accident, I have a hard time when it comes to getting up early in the morning. I can't sit or lay too long, and I can't walk too much. I have to constantly move around to keep my muscles from being stiff.

"How is baby girl treating you?" Tisha asked me.

Since moving down here, we've become close to her. I love everything about her and the way she conducts herself. I was pissed when Legend told me what happened. It's like she stooped low for a nigga that's putting bitches before his girl. That shit is unacceptable. I love Duce like a brother, but he is a dog. He's been this way since they were little. All in high school, he was the class clown and fucked different bitches on a daily.

"Baby boy is doing well?" I said laughing.

Instead of a gender reveal like everyone else was doing, we decided to go back to old school and just wait until the baby is born. As far as clothes and other things, we were buying small portions of everything. I'm still in shock about being pregnant since Aniyah is still so young.

"I'm rooting for a girl," she said, smiling.

"Anyway, what's the deal, hunny? Everybody is working, stacking, and staying out the way. I love it."

"I wish. I just want to reopen my center. I miss getting up every morning." I feel like I'm in a fucked up situation right now.

"I know you do, but your health comes first. If Legend tells you to rest and let him make the money, then don't argue with him. I'm thirty-five, so I know what it's like to want help but never get it. Legend is a real man."

When she said that, I knew she was speaking on the shit Duce had been doing. I grabbed the dog, Aniyah, and pulled her out for a walk around the block.

"Talk to me, boo."

"I fucked up because when we first met, it was based on me being a private investigator for him and his people. One thing led to another, and soon we were fucking on the low. Things started to heat up, and he began buying me these lavish cars and expensive clothes. In my eyes, I'm thinking he could really be the one. I thought moving down here would change the way be thinks about a relationship as a whole." She sniffled and wiped her nose with some napkins.

"Nowadays, you have to let these niggas come to you, and not the other way around. Let them chase you. We all learn a lot in different relationships. I learned Pike was in it for the money that he thought would be his when my father died, and not for love. Being with Legend woke me up. Love will show. Love will keep you happy. Love will expand your dreams as a family, and all that other bullshit will be a distant memory." I hope she got my drift.

"I'm confused."

"Has Duce ever shown you love?"

"No, not really. I think he shows love with gifts and other expensive things." I could tell she was opening her eyes now.

"Duce isn't capable of loving you right now because he's not ready to go in that direction and you are. We as woman tend to allow them to play with other bitches too long and too much until it's too late and love done already hit us. Now, we ready to fight bitches who look him wrong. Your situation is that you shot him instead."

"That's why I know I have to walk away. He got me out here showing my ass, and that's not me. You know how many niggas are checking for a bitch like me. I'm telling you I was about to beat every bitch at the party. If it weren't for Nastasia, I probably would have gone to jail.

"He doesn't see that because he feels he got you locked in and you not going nowhere. You gotta wake up and smell the coffee." She wiped those tears like a strong woman I knew she was.

"You're so lucky to be with Legend."

"Everybody says that, but Legend's past is just as bad as Duce. The thing is Legend gave it up for us. I never begged him or had to argue over a bitch. Even if he is out there fucking with someone, I can bet you they know I'm his everything. I can bet you that he'll get home at a certain time and check on us whenever he's away."

"So, you're ok with him cheating or entertaining another bitch?"

"Hell, naw. What's done in the dark will come to light. I will never stress myself out over something that I don't see. If I do find out that he's cheating, I will walk away and act like what we had was nothing. That's on my dead brothers. I'm getting to a point in my life where there ain't no room to be playing with these niggas." I laid it out and ended the story. I just refuse to be dealing with fuck nigga shit.

"Now that we got that out the way let's go get some lunch. Legend will be out all day working on that mansion and the new project at the apartments."

I had the dog, so I walked him back to the house, and we all drove to this nice and quiet restaurant on the other side of town.

"How are you adapting here? When we first got down here, I was ready to go back. I was missing my brothers like crazy. I just be up at night thinking about the old days. I'm at peace now knowing we have their ashes up here with us now. Plus, when I saw all the opportunities, I figured why not stay."

I knew she left her family to be down here with strangers, so I knew it was hard for her as well.

"I'm adapting very well now that I have a team behind me ready to put in work." She had just opened her a small private investigator firm near the city.

"The more I get out and see Cali for myself, the more I'm learning."

I agreed with her.

Once we sat inside the restaurant, I placed Aniyah in a high chair and ordered our food. We sat and talked about a lot of things and that's when a bitch from the next table started looking my way. The way she looked at me didn't sit well with me. I tried to ignore her because I had my daughter with me.

"Why does she keep looking at me? Do I got a booger on my face?" I said jokingly, but I was offended. She didn't even speak but was intrigued by me.

"The thing that got me ready to bug up is the fact that she is whispering to her friend like we can't see her. Let me jaw this bitch real quick. I'm not about to play with these Cali hoes."

I knew Tisha had a past when it came to the streets. She turned her life around, got a degree, and changed. However, from time to time, she be ready to let loose.

"Naw, don't do it. I got Aniyah, and I'm pregnant. I got a feeling we gone be seeing her again," I said and smiled.

The fact that she was pissed I didn't fall into the trap fucked her head up. I have more respect for myself. We finished eating and went our separate ways. As soon as I was about to get in the car, I heard my name.

"Onari, is that you?" I turned, and it was this dude named Kane. We both went to college together, but he graduated some years before me, and that was that.

"Wassup, Kane? What are you doing down here?"

"Shit, I moved down here after some shit went down with my

brother getting killed. I just couldn't deal with the fact that the guy who did it was out free. I needed some new and fresh air."

"Yea, that was fucked up."

Kane had a brother name Rodrick who was executed and burned to death. The police in Chicago couldn't solve his murder, and it went cold. There were rumors that it was Duce, but I never heard my brothers mention that. Quan would normally tell me everything. I don't even think Kane knew who killed his brother.

"Now I'm here and stacking. I just opened a small club that is doing very good. You need to stop by so that we can catch up."

"As soon as I drop this load, I'm all for it." I smiled, and he hugged me.

Kane and I were always in the computer lab together, which is how we became close. I soon learned he was from the same neighborhood as me, and he became something like a brother to me. He was very laid back and cool.

"Who is the lucky guy? I need to meet him and make sure he's treating you like the queen you are." He laughed and gave me a wink.

"Oh, he's everything I ever wanted in a man," I boasted on Legend because he was my king.

"That's wassup. Take my number down so that we can keep in touch."

"No doubt." We exchanged numbers, and we said goodbye.

For the rest of the day, Aniyah and I stayed at my grandma's house to keep her company.

TWENTY-SIX

NASTASIA

"Troy, oh my god!"

With Troy's head between my legs, I was in heaven. This was his morning routine, and he made sure that I was left satisfied. The feeling that shot through my body and made my toes curl caused my orgasm to triple, and I exploded all over his face and covers.

"I love you so bad," I said still holding onto his dreads.

I got up to return the favor. I don't care what anybody says about a BON (big ole nigga), my baby got a big ass dick and knows how to use it well.

"I love you too, girl."

After we finished making love, we both got up to get our day started. Since moving down here, Troy made sure I was in tune with the streets and what's going on around us. After all that shit happened in Chicago, and the way Quan's death affected them, I couldn't argue. His main thing was trust no one, not even family.

Three days out of the week, we go to the gym like before, and after, we go to the gun range. It took me a while to get the hang of everything and learn how each gun worked, but it's coming along nicely now.

"I don't think we should show her shit. It's gone be deadly. I'm telling you right now, Troy," Duce said as soon as we got out the car. He and Legend were already there to let some steam off. They all were working real hard, and this was a getaway.

"Shut the fuck up before I call Tisha. Oops, I forgot she not fuckin' with you no more." Duce was the irritating brother everyone hated to see coming.

"You and Onari are the reason why she's up here showing out. Y'all gone get her fucked up in Cali."

"Don't blame us. You shouldn't be entertaining these bird brain bitches. Every time I see you or Legend in a bitch's face, I'm tricking. Y'all got us fucked up."

Troy just shook his head because he knew that I was for all the bullshit.

"Leave me out y'all shit," Legend tried to defend himself. I was still pissed a bitch was all in his face. Then he tried to act as if I did something wrong.

"You're the main one already entertaining bitches and passing my number out. Then you got bitches all in ya face. Play if you wanna." He just laughed and waved me off.

"Let's get started and leave the bullshit alone." Troy roughly grabbed my arm and pulled me away.

"Man, stay the fuck out their business. As long as I keep you happy, fuck what they got going on." He gave me the death look. Not wanting to take shit to another level, I let it go and let my anger speak through those bullets.

FOR AN HOUR STRAIGHT, all you could hear were bullets hitting the boards. That alone made me tired, but we didn't stop there. We went another hour before we called it quits. On the way home, he chewed my ass right up.

"The fact that you decided to jump in their business because of some shit Duce said is beyond me. You gotta pipe the fuck down. We moved out here for the better. If Onari feels like Legend is up to no good, that's between them two. Let her figure that shit out on her own. We don't need no extra bullshit going on right now." He made everything perfectly clear.

"I'm not on no bullshit Troy. I'm just tryna make sure this transition wasn't for nothing."

"Are you fucking serious right now? The fact that you think everything we're doing is all a lie is crazy. It's not only me. Legend and Duce also got big plans behind this movement. Aside from the street shit, we gone be at the top real soon. Stop doubting what we got going on."

He was pissed, so I left it alone.

THE NEXT COUPLE OF DAYS, it was just the girls and me basically catching up. Troy was still pissed, so I didn't question shit and let him cool off.

"Catch up with me boo. What's the tea?" Solo asked while Onari, Tisha, and I accompanied him. We were chilling in my Jacuzzi having some cocktails.

"Nothing much. Troy chewed my ass about the drama. Y'all know I don't be on no bullshit unless I smell bullshit. I got a feeling whatever they did in the past will be coming forward. Or it's gone be some messy bitches on bullshit."

"Why you say that?" Onari stopped rubbing her growing belly as if she wanted to hear some shit pertaining to Legend. I didn't even want to tell her that I saw him talking to some girl because I honestly don't know what was said.

"I've been around this shit since I was in my teens, and California was the number one place they had bitches lined up. These hoes were flying to Chicago to see Legend and Troy before we became official. I'm not saying they're doing something, but I gotta keep my eyes open. I'm not about to play these fuck nigga games."

Solo laughed while Tisha nodded her head in agreeance.

"Girl if you don't stop. I'm your cousin, and I won't tell you differently. Don't go opening up doors that can fuck your relationship up. I do know the love they have for y'all is rare, so let's keep the peace. I can't be out here knocking hoes out over y'all men."

We all laughed except Onari. She was rubbing her stomach while looking into space.

"You ok?" I didn't want her to start overthinking. That's why I didn't say shit to her about the incident.

"I have been feeling small pains, but nothing major."

"Naw, we ain't gone do that. Get yo ass up and let's go to the emergency room. My niece or nephew will not be in harm's way."

I was serious. Ever since Legend lost his baby at birth, I could see the pain in his eyes. He wanted to be a daddy so bad, and it seemed like everything went downhill from there.

"It's nothing. I just felt a small little bump. It's probably a kick."

"Ok. Promise me that you will go if it keeps continuing."

"I will." She smiled and began texting on her phone. Whoever it was had her attention, and I knew it wasn't Legend because he would call her.

"Bitch, you must want your ears stomped together?"

"What?" she was looking confused.

"Who the fuck are you texting?"

"Girl, this guy named Kane. I went to school with him years ago, but he graduated before me. I saw him up here the other day. It's nothing."

That didn't sound good, but like Troy said to stay out of it, so I shrugged it off.

"Ok. What y'all doing this Saturday. My homies having a barbecue with all the liquor, weed, and food we could get for free. What's up?" Solo was a party animal and never sat down.

"I think Troy was talkin' about going," I said, sipping my drink.

"I'm down," Tisha said like she was ready to throw her ass around.

"Count me in. It ain't much I can do but eat," Onari said with a big smile. Food always made her happy.

"Don't even ask me. If it's music and drinks, I'm there."

We all began singing to Anita Baker since she was playing in the background. Times like this I look forward to because it's like we rarely see each other since we all have our own families.

TWENTY-SEVEN

LEGEND

I was currently riding in my light green Cadillac through these Cali streets bumping that old Do or Die "Foreign". Shit has been going real good for a nigga. Making this move was one of the best things I did since getting out. The only thing I'm waiting on now is my baby to be born and to ask Onari to marry me. I always promised myself that when shit is in order, anything is possible. I'm also looking forward to putting my name on paperwork saying that Aniyah is officially mine. I love that little girl like she was mine.

Pulling up to the corner store, I instantly ran into the chick Samantha. I had just seen her at Duce's card party, and she was on it. I wasn't on shit, but apparently Nastasia thought I was. It's like everywhere I went, there she is. I knew she was selling pussy because anywhere money is involved, she right there shaking her ass. Around the corner was this big ass barbecue Big Tone was throwing, so I'm sure she was going to be there. I jumped out and ran inside to get me some swishers and a fifth of Rémy.

"Damn Legend, you riding clean around this bitch. Let me hop in and check that bitch out." I gave her ass a look like stop fronting yo moves. We ain't even on that type of level.

"Naw, I'm good." I calmly said and walked inside the store. Niggas already knew me, so my name being mentioned wasn't a surprise.

"Legend, my man. How's life treating you? I heard that you and your beautiful wife are expecting?" Nitty was the crackhead everyone helped out because he was always down to ride.

"Wassup, Nitty. Life's good, and I couldn't ask for a better wife. She is my everything." I boasted on my Onari. I'm sure everyone in town knew who she was.

"That's wassup. Keep your eyes open and your ears to these streets. You know I got you, bro."

We shook up, and I jumped back in my car after paying for my stuff. When I pulled up to the barbecue, most of the guys were already there, including some faces I never saw.

"This nigga pull up in a Now and Later ass Cadi. Fuck you think you doing?"

Big Tone and I had history. It was an honor to roll up on his shit with million dollar colors. Back in the day, we used to go toe to toe with our cars. The better cars always had the better bitches, and most of the time, I won.

"You see me taking over, nigga." I laughed and shook up with every one of the guys. Of course, Duce was shacked up with the same bitch who got his windows busted. He ain't gone learn.

Most of the females out and about weren't familiar to me, so that was a good thing. I was trying to bury my past and not let it come into my future. That shit can be deadly. The whole time we were drinking and partying, I noticed this dude constantly looking at me. I had to keep my eyes on him because I didn't trust a soul out here in these streets.

"You know dude?" Duce was on game just like me.

"Naw, but he gone soon find out if he don't acknowledge who the fuck he is." I drunk down my whole cup of liquor and poured another.

"Ah, hell naw, which one of you niggas invited them?" Duce said, and I turned to see what the fuck he was talking about.

Onari, Tisha, Nastasia, and Solo were getting out of the car. The crazy part was that Onari was driving my brand new Benz, which I barely drove. I had just left the house, and she didn't mention anything about coming here. That shit didn't sit well with me.

"So that's what we doing? We making moves without letting each other know?" I said when I walked up to her.

My baby was looking good as fuck in a fitted one-piece jogging suit. It hugged all her curves, including that ass and her baby bump. The fact that she was even out here looking this good while she was pregnant pissed me off.

"You've been making moves without telling me. I'm just returning the favor." The way she said it let me know something else was bugging her mind.

"Yo, watch out, man. Come talk to me." I wasn't feeling this shit.

"Legend, chill with ya boys. I'm not on anything. I just needed to get out and get some air." I wasn't feeling how she was coming at me.

"I guess," I said, and she went back over to where Solo and the rest of them were. I just ignored the bullshit and finished drinking.

THROUGHOUT THE NIGHT, it started to get crowded, so I looked for Onari so we could head home. When I spotted her near the food tables talking to the same dude that was watching me, all my thoughts floated above my head. I instantly pulled my gun out and made some fucking noise around this bitch.

POW! POW!

"Legend! What the fuck?" I heard Nastasia say, and before I could get to Onari, they all tried to block her in. If anybody knew me, they knew what I was capable of doing. Buddy ass took off running, so I couldn't even get to his ass.

"Get in the fucking car yo," I calmly said while eyeballing the fuck out of her. With my gun still out, she didn't have a choice. As she began to walk slowly, the crowd began to leave, and Duce and Troy walked up.

"Bro, calm down." Troy tried to take the gun.

"Ain't no fucking calm down. My bitch out here chatting with some off the wall ass nigga like I'm some lame ass nigga in the streets. Does she not know who the fuck Legend is around this bitch?" I began looking for dude, but he was ghost.

Everyone that knew me began getting in their cars. Onari got in my Cadi, and I tossed my keys to Nastasia letting her know she was driving the Benz back home.

As soon as I got inside, I cut the radio all the way up and pulled away at full speed of fifty miles per hour. She had me fucked up.

"Legend, can you please slow down?" I could see the fear in her eyes. It wasn't intentional, but I needed to know who the fuck that lame ass dude was and why he was all in her face.

"Who the fuck is dude? You better start talking or I'ma light California up starting with you and him."

"I went to school with him, nothing more."

"Fuck is you smiling all in his face for? Do I not make you happy?"

"Really, Legend?"

"Do I not make you happy?"

"Yes," she said while pulling her phone out. She had the shit on silent, but I could see the flashing lights, so I knew someone was calling. I snatched it from her, and a nigga named Kane popped up. I tossed it back and told her to answer.

"What?"

"Answer it before I blow your shit right off." She was shaking like a leaf when I pulled my gun from my waist and placed it to her head. She had me fucked up.

"Hello." I made her put it on speaker.

"Are you ok?" he asked, and I answered for his bitch ass.

"My wife is good, playboy. Find another bitch to play with. No more warnings." I simply stated, and he hung up.

She just sat with tears coming down her face as if I embarrassed her. She had me fucked up. My name ring bells all through this bitch, but when they attach another nigga with it, we have problems. As soon as we pulled up in the driveway, she jumped out and tried to hurry inside.

"ONARI!" I called her name, but she ignored me, put the code in the door, and walked inside. I was seeing blood.

When I walked inside, Ms. Rosie was sitting on the couch with Aniyah sleep next to her.

"Is everything ok?"

"Yea, no worries." I laid my keys on the table and skipped up the stairs.

The feeling that was going through my body was not good. Just the fact that this nigga had her number didn't sit well with me. When I walked into the room and slammed the door, she tried to run in the bathroom, but I stopped her.

"My motherfuckin' name ain't Legend for shit. I think you forgot what I'm capable of in these streets." I grabbed her by that one piece she was wearing and pinned her on the bed.

"Legend, stop." she tried to fight me off, but it didn't work.

"Let this be a fuckin' lesson. The next time I see another nigga in your face, shit ain't gone end well. I will end your fuckin' life before I let you disrespect me." I got up off her and walked out the room. Nastasia and Solo were outside the door.

"Did you hit her, Legend?" Nastasia jumped in my face, and I pushed her back.

"Ok, that's enough. Let him get some air. Onari is gone be ok." Ms. Rosie came up the stairs and pulled them away from me. I couldn't think at the moment, so I grabbed my keys and left.

A COUPLE OF DAYS LATER, this shit was hitting me hard. Onari had me in a place where I've never been. I had feelings in previous relationships but not like this, not to the point where I'm clowning in the streets.

"When are you going home?" my momma asked me while I was rolling up a blunt at her table. Since I walked out a couple of days ago, I have been all over the place.

"I don't know." I had just finished my work for the day and was tired as fuck. The mansion we've been working on is almost done, so the next project is coming up.

"You need to be at home with her, Legend. She is high risk and could go in labor any day." I heard this every day from her. I know she was tired of me, so after I smoked, I grabbed my shit and went to Duce's crib.

I should have been going home, but I just couldn't right now. I was more fucked up that she didn't call me.

"Nigga, you still homeless?" Duce started cracking jokes when I walked inside his house.

The moment I saw three bitches laid out across his couch, I should have turned around. One of the bitches was Samantha, and she was enjoying herself to the fullest.

"If you don't want another ass shot you better leave me alone." He laughed then handed me a Corona and some more weed. I knew shit was heating up when one of the girls began dancing all in my face. She had a fat ass, but her face wasn't it. Then, Samantha joined in, and I knew I should have left.

"You a cute light skinned nigga. Chicago got it on the money side too." The other girl was licking her lips, and at that point, my dick started to jump.

When they pulled me into the back room, I didn't have to do shit. They both dropped to their knees and gave a nigga some sloppy ass head — one on the balls, and the other sucking my dick. At first, I wasn't feeling it, but when I felt that sensation shoot through my body, I let it all loose.

"I need some dick now," Samantha blurted out when I started to pull my pants up. I started to feel guilty, so I calmly walked out of the room.

"Onari just went to the hospital. You need to get there, asap." I ran smack into Solo. My heart dropped, and I couldn't even put on a front. When the girl came out of the room, he laughed and walked out.

"You done fucked up now," Duce said, throwing salt on the situation. All I could do was shake my head and go straight to the hospital.

TWENTY-EIGHT
ONARI

"Mama," I heard and slowly sat up in the bed.

It was nine in the morning, and of course, Aniyah was up. I couldn't sleep anyway because I was having small pains here and there, so I turned the TV to cartoons for her. Since Legend's been gone, I felt sick on the inside. I was constantly crying tryna figure out what went wrong. I've seen him lash out plenty of times, but never have I ever thought he would come towards me. The look in his eyes when he saw me talking to Kane was a look I never want to see again.

"Hey, how are you?" My grandma hasn't been home since I called and told her I wasn't feeling too well.

"I'm a little sore, but other than that, I'm ok." I had cried so much, my eyes were puffy, and I wasn't really eating.

"I think you should go to the hospital. I don't care what you and Legend got going on, that baby is still more important."

"I know," I said and decided to soak in the tub. I needed to clear my head.

The whole time I was inside the tub, I was starting to feel sick. Once I washed up, I slowly got up and felt dizzy to the point that I almost fell. Once I stepped out the tub, water gushed out and down my legs, and at the same time, I threw up.

"Grandma!" I called her name while sitting on the floor.

"Oh my god!" She rushed inside to make sure that I was ok.

"I think my water bag busted."

"Are you sure?"

"I don't know." I was scared because the doctors warned me not to get in the tub once I hit six months and because I was high risk.

"Come on. We gotta get you to the hospital. I'ma call Legend so that he can meet us there."

She helped me up off the floor, and I dried off and threw some jogging pants and a t-shirt on. As I looked down at my feet, I noticed they were swollen, so I grabbed my Moccasin's to put on.

"Legend didn't answer, so his mom is on her way to get Aniyah. Do you got everything you need?"

"I just need my wallet and phone," I told her. I made sure to grab a bag because I had a sick feeling to my stomach.

Once Legend's mom came, my grandma and I went straight to the hospital. As soon as I walked inside, I threw up inside the bag. The nurse on duty called for a doctor, and they rushed me in the back.

"Do you feel any pain, Ms. Williams?" They were hooking me up to all these machines to monitor the baby.

"It keeps coming and going," I said, remembering how that shit felt from when I had Aniyah.

"Ok, don't worry. Right now, we gone work on your blood pressure going down and making sure your baby is ok." I was scared, so I know that was a big factor in my baby's health.

AFTER A COUPLE of hours and a little sleep, I woke up to Nastasia sitting next to me.

"Where is Legend?" I expected him to be here, but he wasn't.

"Here, sit up and eat." My grandma had a ham sandwich for me.

"I'm not hungry."

"Yes, you are. The doctors will be in shortly to give you the news." Nastasia helped me sit up, and she was trying to avoid my question. My heart started racing.

"He should be here soon."

I grabbed my phone and began texting him. I was pissed.

Babe: *The fact that I been here all day and you haven't called or even came here. Fuck you yo!*

I slammed the phone down and slowly began eating my food.

"Hi, Ms. Williams. We've been monitoring the baby and as of right now, the baby is ready to come, but I'm not. I don't want to risk your life, so we're going to help you hold the baby inside of you as long as we can. What you were feeling was small contractions, but we stopped them."

"So how long before she can deliver?" my grandma asked him.

"If we can get her to the nine-month mark, then we can definitely deliver. She just hit eight months so I would like to keep her here to monitor them both. When we checked your blood pressure, it was extremely high, not to mention you had a slight fever when you walked inside. That was why you were throwing up. I'm not sure if you're aware, but stress can cause you to go in labor early. We have to keep you here to make sure everything is ok."

I couldn't argue. At the same time, my phone began blowing up. Opening my Facebook, I received pictures of Legend and Duce. When I got the picture of the females, I almost threw up. The same bitch that was watching me in the restaurant was all in the picture. I specifically looked at the date, and it was a couple of hours ago that this happened. This is why he wasn't responding to our calls. Once the doctor left, I handed the phone to Nastasia. Trying to hold the tears, it was no use.

"How could he? I fucking hate him, yo."

Neither Nastasia nor my grandma could defend him this time. I knew he was still pissed at what happened at the barbecue, but he was dead wrong. To go out and kick it with the next bitch was a low blow.

"I'm tryna figure out why she messaged you that shit. She's a messy ass bitch." I could see Nastasia messaging her back, but I stopped her.

"It's ok. I don't even wanna entertain this bitch." I was getting ready to delete and block her altogether, but when she posted *when the dick is good and got a nice birthmark on it, I'm in love.* I knew then that he fucked her.

"I'm so done with him. I don't even want him here. He can come when I deliver the baby." The tears wouldn't stop flowing.

"You don't mean that. You're upset right now, and that's not good for that baby. You heard what that doctor said." My grandma rubbed my head to calm me down.

"What did I do wrong?" Nastasia handed me some napkins to wipe my face. I was already self-conscience about my skin, and now it's as if maybe I'm not good enough.

"Nothing. Don't ever think you did anything wrong. He fucked up, not you."

It took a minute, but I eventually calmed down. I had to tell myself that this is not me. I have never in my life felt some type of way over any nigga. I am that bitch. Niggas dream of a bitch like me on a daily. My only problem was I fucked up by letting him pull me all the way to Cali when he had a fucking past, a past I'm not sure I want to even run into.

"Solo and Legend are coming up now," Nastasia said. I assumed one of them sent her a text.

"I don't want him in here with me. I swear I'ma snap," I said, pulling my hair up into a tight bun and getting out the bed not caring that I had tubes all through my arms. I was ready to fight his ass. I guess it was too late. He came walking into my room, and he knew he fucked up. His face said it all. Guilt was all through his eyes.

"I fucking hate you! Get him out of here." If my grandma weren't standing in between us, I would have slapped his ass.

"Chill, ma. I'm sorry." Solo and Nastasia pulled him out of the room before the doctors came in.

"I don't want him near me. I don't even want him around my kids. Grandma, I need you to pack some things and take them to your house. I'm done," I said, getting back in the bed.

"You gone be ok," was all my grandma told me. I knew I would be, but this shit hurt so bad.

A COUPLE OF DAYS LATER, I had to deal with multiple text messages and Legend constantly calling my phone. The thing Legend didn't realize was that I wasn't like them birdbrain bitches that he used to fuck. I can love you today and act like you're dead tomorrow. That's exactly what I was doing.

"Girl, he's going crazy over you."

My grandma wanted me to talk to him so bad, but I couldn't. That shit was still fresh in my mind. The thought of him loving on a bitch the same way he does me is mind-boggling. Then I knew it was spiteful on the bitch's side because she was mugging me hard in the restaurant.

"He did this, not me." I was about to take a walk around the hospital, which was recommended by the doctors. Once they got everything under control, they didn't want me to sit around and make my pregnancy hard, movement was a must.

"I know, but think about all the good he has done. He's a really good guy. Y'all need to figure this all out. I'm not taking no for an answer," she said matter of factly.

"I'ma be downstairs smoking me a cigarette. Do yo rounds and clear ya head. You've been doing good these last couple of days, so keep it up."

We both walked out of the room, and she went downstairs while I walked around the hospital. I walked for about thirty minutes before I returned to the room. As soon as I got to the door,

I noticed the smell of his cologne. That shit was so strong, not to mention one of my favorites. I had to brace myself before I walked inside.

"Look, ma. I just wanna tell you how sorry I am. I never meant to hurt you." He was practically on his knees begging me to forgive him.

If my mind were only on fucking at the moment, I would give in because he was looking real daddyish at the moment. Those jogging suits that gave his dick a nice print was not good at the moment. I had to snap back and remember why I was still pissed.

"Did you fuck her?" I got right to the point.

"No. I swear I didn't." He had some flowers in his hand.

"It's funny because she made sure to mention that birthmark on yo dick." I couldn't help but laugh.

"They sucked my dick on some drunk shit. That was it." He tried to touch me, but I moved away from him.

"They?" I questioned because I thought it was only one.

"Please, Onari."

"That makes it ok? Because they were drunk, you're telling me all of this is a pass. You were drunk too and enjoyed every bit of it." I looked at him as if he had two heads.

"No, but I promise this shit wasn't planned yo. After that shit at the barbecue, I snapped. My mind was all fucked up."

"No, your mind was fucked up because you jumped to conclusions. You took it upon yourself to think I was fucking him. Kane and I went to college together. Other than that, we have no history. No, he has never come on to me, even at the barbecue. The fact that you walked away from us for a couple of days and end up with a bitch that got diarrhea at the mouth hurt me so bad. So bad to the point that I realized it's not worth it. You got me fucked up, Legend. I don't give a fuck what you did in the past with those bitches. I'm supposed to be your future."

Once again, the tears started rolling.

"It wasn't like that. I have never been in love before. You got my nose wide open, and now I can't think straight without you by my side. I'm going crazy without you. I know I fucked up, but don't do me like this, yo."

I wiped the tears because I was doing fine until he got here.

"Stress in me is not good. I came in here with a fever, and blood pressure high. I just need you to leave me alone right now."

He didn't argue or anything. He simply sat the flowers down and walked towards the door.

"This ain't the end of us. I'ma give you some more space," he said and walked out the door.

LATER THAT DAY, my contraction skyrocketed, and the baby heart monitor started beeping. When the doctors came inside, I was told that they would be doing an emergency C-Section.

TWENTY-NINE

DUCE

When Legend told me about the dude that was all in Onari's face, I did my own investigation. I called Tisha for help, but she wasn't fucking with me anymore, not even on the business side.

"What you find out?"

Legend and I were at the gym tryna let some steam off. He was going through a thing after what happened. I felt bad knowing shit wasn't supposed to be like that. I knew Onari was different because he was constantly talking about her and the way he hurt her. The bitch that posted that shit went ghost because she knew she fucked up. That's why I fuck with bitches who be in and out, bitches from other cities on that one-night stand type of shit. She was a hood bitch from the beginning, so that's where we fucked up at. The crazy part was that Legend had already fucked Samantha years ago. I don't understand why she thinks shit was different now. We didn't even have a fucking Facebook, so she put that shit on her page on some hating shit. I hate a thirsty bitch.

"The only thing I found out was that we had ties to his brother."

"We had ties to a lot of niggas. Who?"

"Rodrick."

When I said that, he raised his eyebrow. Rodrick was the nigga I killed a couple of years ago for stunting on our click like we were some bitches. Real niggas don't move like that. He wasn't a real nigga, So he had to go. I did that man so dirty that the police couldn't even identify him. They had to use dental records and fingerprints.

"We definitely have to keep our eyes open. Shit is not sitting well with me. The fact that he went to college in Chicago with her, and now all of a sudden he's in Cali, I'm not stupid."

Legend was texting Onari, but I figured she didn't respond. She was sending my man into a fucking hole. He was depressed.

"I feel you. Whatever is going on, I don't think Onari is aware of it."

"I don't give a fuck. I warned his ass once. The next time I'ma let my bullets do the talking. Those warning shots should have opened his eyes. Instead, the nigga called her while we were in the car."

I laughed because this was not like him. Legend never gave a fuck about a bitch until now. Onari got my mans out here acting a fool.

"Beat that hoe's head in when you see her. I'm all for slapping hoes," I said, referring to Samantha.

"Bro, we ain't finna put our hands on no bitch, but Nastasia will." Nastasia was our go to when bitches were tryna cut up. I should have let her and Tisha beat Samantha's ass at my card party.

"She's pissed at you right now."

"When ain't she pissed? She's gone be alright."

We worked out some more until we got tired. As soon as I walked out to my car, I spotted Tisha getting out her car. She has been avoiding my calls, and I wasn't for none of the bullshit. Seeing other men watch her ass while she was bent over fucked me all the way up.

"So, you gone keep avoiding me, right?" She was looking real edible at the moment. I forgot how fat her ass was.

"Donte, please. You got what you wanted now leave me alone." She grabbed her gym bag and began to walk away.

"Man, you got me fucked up."

"You got yourself fucked up. I'm not that bitch, bro."

"Bro? Who the fuck you calling bro?" I was ready to smash her shit in the ground at that moment. I was on good bullshit, so before Legend pulled off, he talked some sense in my ass.

"You just got shot in the ass by her. Leave her alone." He got in between us before I slap slob out her mouth.

"Fuck her."

As I turned back around to get in my car, both of our phones began blowing up. Seeing the messages from Troy telling us Onari went into labor made us both hop in the car. I hope this wasn't another false alarm.

"I'ma follow you there," I told him, and he said ok. The look on his face was priceless. My mans was about to be a father for the first time.

THE MOMENT we walked into the hospital, everyone was already there. Legend told the doctors who he was, and they immediately took him to the back.

"I thought she wasn't due yet?" I knew she was having complications, but shit got serious now.

"She started having severe pains, and when the doctor checked her, the baby was tryna come on out," Ms. Rosie said while we patiently waited in the hallway.

"I know my god baby better come out healthy," I said, and they all looked at me weird.

"How you just gone say your god baby? Who established this?" Nastasia said on some hating shit.

"Me, now mind ya business." They all laughed.

WE WAITED another hour before the doctors walked out to give us the news.

"How did everything go?" Ms. Rosie was so happy.

"Everything went well for mom, but the baby isn't breathing on her own. She stopped breathing once we pulled her out, but we now have her stabilized. Right now, we're running test to make sure nothing else is at risk. She was born too soon, and because of that, she will be here for a while." When he said she, I knew Legend got his girl.

"Praise the Lord. I know my grandbaby was gone be ok. She got my strong blood running through those veins," she blurted out. After all the shit we've been through as a whole, this news was everything.

"I'm voting on Emily. I like that name," I said, and Troy put his two cents in.

"Who the fuck is Emily?"

"My god baby's name. That's what I'ma name her."

"You are tripping. That must be your bitch's name." Nastasia stays starting bullshit.

"Legend already said I could name her. You're just mad." Everyone was cracking up at us.

"Well, I'm naming her Briana."

"Get that thot ass name out of here. She ain't finna be thottin' like y'all were. Yo name says a lot about you." She picked up a pencil and threw it at me.

"I hate yo ass."

"We're equal then." We talked for a little bit more, and then all of a sudden about three police officers walked inside.

"Donte Ackins. You're under arrest for the murder of Patrick Jones. Whatever you say can and will be used against you in the court of law," was all I heard before I zoned out.

We had killed Pike months ago right before we left Chicago. They recently found some of his body where we left it, and his baby momma has been running her mouth to the law. I knew they would find me, so I was prepared for whatever.

"Troy, call my lawyer," I said before they walked me to the car. I wasn't saying shit until my lawyer got there. They already knew that and didn't even mention an interview.

THEY HAD me waiting for almost three hours and tried to offer me food and water. I declined and chose to starve to death because I know how the system works.

"Man, get me out of here," I said as soon as my lawyer walked in. He handed me some food from McDonald's, which I didn't care for, but anything will do right now. He knew me well and knew I wouldn't eat shit they offered me.

"We're working on it right now. Answer whatever they ask you. I got my people investigating on the outside."

"Did you call Tisha?" I didn't want her name attached to any of this because she was the one that gave us the scoop on Pike and Nytrell.

"She was informed to lay low. Legend got the news, so everyone is aware of what's happening. Don't worry. This will be over before you know it," he reassured me. I knew he would do a damn good job because we pay him bands to get us out of jams like this.

When I finished my food, he took it and put it in his bag so that I wouldn't leave DNA around.

"Mr. Mackie, we've been looking for you," Some detective named Reynolds said while sitting down.

"I wasn't too far," I replied, and he quickly slid me some pictures. It was pictures of the crime scene from the warehouse. Hanging from the ceiling was a burnt body.

"What's this?" I kept my composure so that they couldn't read me.

"This was the work of you and Legend. I have known about y'all since day one. Too bad for you a witness pointed you out." I raised my eyebrow because I know he was bullshitting me.

"Can't be me. Can't be. Start yo investigation over. I'm done talking. I'ma let my lawyer handle it from here," I told them, and they were pissed. I know they didn't think I was gone confess to this shit.

Once my lawyer and I finished talking, I knew Legend would have to put in work to get me out this jam. What was crazy is that they didn't arrest him. Now I know a rat is lurking real close to us. They handcuffed me again and hauled me off to jail.

THIRTY

LEGEND

"I got you, ma. I got you." I held Onari's hand while they were getting ready to cut her open.

When I got the text from Troy telling me that Onari was in labor, I flew to the hospital in my workout clothes. My heart was beating fast because this was the moment everyone been telling me about. I was scared, but at the same time, I was ready to bring my baby in this crazy world.

"Don't let me die, babe." Onari was scared herself, but with the help of the doctors, motivation was everything.

"We got this. I ain't leaving until you and my baby are good. You hear me."

"Yes." The tears were running down her face, and I wiped them while caressing her head. I was already suited up, so now we were ready for this to be over.

"Father God I ask you to look over my fiancée and baby while they go through this horrible ordeal. Heal their bodies, mind, and soul and allow them to continue to make you proud in this crazy world. Amen."

We all said amen, and they began the C-section.

When I saw all the blood, I didn't know it would be like that. I wanted to throw up and run at the same time. Now I know what they say when talking about strong women. You have to be strong to go through shit like this. Having a kid is like dying in a sense.

"Dad cut the umbilical cord," the doctors said once the baby was fully out.

I cut it, and they quickly placed her on a machine. I was nervous because we didn't hear a cry or anything. After about five minutes, the doctors alerted us.

"Baby girl is fine," he blurted over his head while pressing buttons on the machine and attaching tubes through her body. He then wheeled her out into the baby unit.

"You got what you wanted," Onari said while smiling. I just leaned down to kiss her lips.

"I know ma, and I thank you from the bottom of my heart for giving me a gift I always wanted."

She cried because I know she been through a lot and the fact that my recent actions added on to it hit me hard. From the moment we made it official, I promised that I wouldn't hurt her. I didn't live up to my word, and at this point, she might not even take a nigga back.

We waited another thirty minutes before we got the news that baby girl wasn't breathing on her own.

"Is my baby gone be ok?" I asked the doctor when he came to talk to us.

"She is a fighter. Her breathing wasn't good when she came out, so right now she's using a tube to help her breath better. All of her organs are fine, except for one of her lungs. Her right lung is very weak, but don't worry, she will be ok. Before we go into details about the dos and don'ts, I just want you two to enjoy this moment. One of the nurses will take you to the room where she's being kept and keep you updated."

"Thanks so much," I said while still holding Onari's hand. They were stitching her back up and cleaning up the area.

After I went to wipe off, I came back out, and Onari was sitting in a wheelchair. She was still numb, so I'm sure she didn't feel any pain at the moment.

"Her name? We didn't give her a name," she said, and I started thinking. All this time we never discuss a name for a girl because a boy would have been a Jr.

"Princess, my very first princess," I said, and she didn't argue. Princess was her name, and now we were ready to see her.

When they wheeled us out of the room, I noticed the commotion from our family in the waiting area. I couldn't worry about that right now, so I sent Troy a text. He let me know that Duce got lock up for Pike's murder. I didn't even tell Onari. Right now was a good moment, so whatever just happened, I will deal with it later.

Once we got into the room, hearing the beeping sound from the monitor made this shit real. Looking down at her in the incubator, a nigga got soft as fuck. My eyes got watery just seeing all these tubes inside her body.

"Daddy's Princess." I stuck my finger through the hole and touched her little hands.

"She has your big ass head," Onari said, and I laughed.

"That's ok. She's gone be knocking niggas right and left." My Princess was a light bright. It's like she had no color in her skin, but of course, they ran some test, and she was ok.

"She doesn't have no hair."

"That's cuz yo bald head ass gave her those genes," I replied, and she hit my arm. She knew I was fucking with her.

"I'ma grow her hair out like I did Aniyah. She's gone be good."

We literally watched her for two hours, until Onari started feeling the meds wearing off. We got her back to the room so that she could get her rest. I was right by her bedside just to let her know that she wasn't in this alone. I had already given Troy the green light to handle our business when it came to the projects and money. As for Duce getting locked, up, we were already on it with the lawyers.

DAYS LATER, I was in and out of the hospital making sure that everything was there for when baby girl comes home. I also wanted to make sure Onari was comfortable, so I went all out. Today Duce goes in to see the judge, but I needed to know exactly what was said, so I linked up with the lawyer.

"Wassup, Legend? How is it being a new father?" our lawyer said while giving me a handshake. He was suited up ready to go to work, and I wasn't mad.

"Everything is ok for now. I'm just hoping and praying that my baby girl is ok, and she doesn't need to have surgery." He could sense that something was wrong, so he asked me.

"You fucked up, didn't you?" He laughed.

"Hell yea, fucking with Duce. I should have known being around him at that time was not good."

"Duce is a wild animal. We all know that, but you're different Legend. You should have talked to your girl and fixed whatever the problem was. I got faith in both of y'all. As of right now, I need your head in the game. I need you and Troy to stay focused and keep your eyes opened. I'ma talk to Trisha and see if she's still willing to help, but I won't get my hopes up. I got a backup, so we're still good."

"What's the news?" I was ready to hear whatever.

"Duce is being charged with first-degree murder. We already know who it is. The real question is the female that's brought this whole thing to the light. How much does she really know?" I knew he was talking about Pike's other baby momma. The same chick that had her son in Onari's daycare that whole time and Onari never knew. Now I'm starting to think something is wrong. Right after we left, we heard rumors that she was running her mouth and telling people we killed him.

"I've been in this game too long not to know when someone close to me is with the shits," I told him, and he smiled.

"I did some research and remembered that dude that was in Onari's face? Well apparently, he has a baby by Pike's girl as well. In fact, they've been dealing with each other heavy since Pike's death."

I was now confused.

"So she got a kid by Pike and Kane. We got dealings with Kane's brother that you already know of, and now you're telling me they are working together to bring us down? The game has just begun," I said, rubbing my hands together.

I knew it was a reason that nigga was all in my girl's face. Then I believe that bitch was a snake from the beginning.

"Before you get hyped, you're still on parole. I advise you to make a trip to see your parole officer and let him know the good news. As of right now, he doesn't know you're in California. I just need you to stay clear of the bullshit. The first fuck up and you're going back for the remaining three years left on your sentence. You got a family now, Legend. I'm speaking from experience and not just your lawyer. I'ma talk to Duce as well. Let's go inside." He was absolutely right, but I'm not feeling this whole setup. I have to approach it another way.

THIRTY-ONE

NASTASIA

After being with Onari and my new niece for a couple of days, I'm drained now. All I want is my bed, but of course, more bullshit keeps popping up. Now Duce is in jail, and we've got the police following us all around. This shit is mind-boggling.

"All I know is that I'm not answering shit," Solo said like he's been around this shit.

"Solo, you haven't been in the hood since you were little. Stop the bullshit," I said, laughing.

We were chilling at the park letting my son and Aniyah run around. I was caring for her until Ms. Rosie comes back from the hospital. Since Onari had the baby a couple of days ago, they've been keeping an eye on her making sure her body properly heals. She still has scars from the accident that was just closing up.

"I guess you right. I'm still not opening my mouth. They are barking up the wrong tree." He sipped his cooler, and I did the same.

"Look who popped up. I guess life has been much better for you." I said, getting up to hug Tisha. The day she walked away from Duce, I knew she would get her mojo back. The question was, who is this dude she's rolling with.

"Hey y'all. This is my good friend, Lester. These are my other good friends," she said, smiling.

I didn't question shit. Like Troy told me. Mind my business. We welcomed him with open arms, and he seemed pretty cool.

"So how is everything with Onari? I know she's still hurting." Tisha has been back working a lot, so I was ready to fill her in.

"Onari is very strong. She is holding up because she just had the baby, but believe me when I tell y'all she is not who y'all think she is. That was my friend before she was his girl. When you hurt her, she always gets even. We just gotta keep our eyes open because Legend has probably busted a nerve tryna figure out her next moves," I said, laughing.

"Bitch, I don't have time to be playing mind games with his ass. You saw what happened at the barbecue. He fired warning shots. The next time won't be a warning."

Solo was against everything, but I wasn't. Legend will get whatever comes his way, so I'm for all the bullshit.

"Well, right now we need to keep her away from the bullshit. I know how it feels to wanna spazz. The good thing is that I have no kids and she does. We got her back though," Tisha said, smiling.

That's what I loved about my girls. No one knows when we will snap. Only we know when shit like that will pop off, and at that moment were there to pick up the pieces. I know my girl is hurting, so I gotta get her back to herself.

THE NEXT MORNING, I was up bright and early, ready to take Aniyah to Ms. Rosie. Troy was cooking breakfast, so I knew something was on his mind. He is barely home to eat.

"Good morning, babe. Talk to me." I sat at the table while he fixed the kids and me a plate.

"I've just been thinking about Duce and all the shit that's going on. When Legend went to jail, I realized life ain't what it used to be.

We ran these streets, babe. We gave the lil niggas a chance to get money in a positive way while we were getting money the illegal way. All I wanted was a life I never had. Once I got it, I realized everything comes with a price. I lost my family in a shootout, and I could never get them back. I know it's been almost eight years, but I don't ever want that shit to happen to me again. All I'm trying to do is be here for my son and you. Everything else doesn't matter. At this point, I don't even wanna be a part of the shit Duce got going on."

This was the first time I heard him speak like this, especially when he spoke of his sister and mom getting killed in a crossfire years ago.

"What are your plans going forward?" I kept calm because I wasn't sure where this conversation was going.

"I'm not sure. I just don't want to sleep with one eye opened anymore. I moved here so that we can be at ease and not worry about fuck niggas coming at us. I know him getting locked up was for some shit that happened in Chicago, but overall when do this shit stop. We lost Quan, and we lost Trell. I feel like the day Trell chose those drugs was the day he signed his death certificate. All I want is for all of us to get on the same page and leave the bullshit where we left it."

I could see that he was stressed. This whole ordeal has been stressful, but I know we didn't come all the way here to give up.

"Just know that I got us. Whatever happens, we gone overcome it and keep pushing. Overall, I think you should have that man to man talk with Duce. Find out his state of mind. There might be something deep going on that no one knows about. You feel me?"

"Yea, I feel you. I'ma have that talk with him. Thanks, ma." I smiled because our conversations are everything.

After we all ate breakfast, I got Aniyah's bag, and we headed out the door.

"I love you, babe!" I yelled over my shoulders.

"Love you too, girl." Troy watched us until I pulled out the driveway and headed to the hospital.

Once I got there, I handed Aniyah over to Ms. Rosie and decided to sit with Onari.

"Wassup, new mommy? How is my niece doing?" I walked in her room, and she was standing by the window just looking out.

"I remember when I was little, and I used to sit at home and wait by the window until my dad got off work. I used to play with my dolls and wouldn't dare move because I wanted him to see me waiting for him. That man was my everything. He was my king."

She ignored my question and turned around. The tears coming down her cheeks showed me how hurt my girl really was. I slowly walked up to her and grabbed her hands.

"I thought losing my dad would kill me. Nope. I had my two big brothers. They kept me sane and were my protectors. I would brag about them to everyone and dare someone step to me," she smirked.

"Then there was Legend. He was there when I lost my brothers. I thought I would die. He told me that he would protect me from any hurt or evil thing coming my way. Nope. He was the one that hurt me, Nastasia. Out of everybody in my life, I didn't expect this so soon. I trusted him and look at me."

I just pulled her in for a hug. The tears fell down my cheeks as wells.

"What are your plans now?" I asked her because as women, we have to stand up. We can't keep letting men take control of our lives and feelings.

"I think I'ma step back so that I can focus on my kids and me now. I need to get my head back in the game and get my daycare back up and running. I just need some air and space." She wiped her tears.

"I told yo ass about all that crying. Now I'm crying and I'ma thug. Thugs don't cry." We both broke out laughing.

"Whatever you decide, I got your back," I said, hugging her.

"Thanks, boo. To answer your question, Princess is doing good. She started breathing on her own, so they removed the tubes, but she will still need to stay here until her weight picks up."

"She's gone be home in no time. As of right now, we need to stay clear of the police. They on good bullshit since Duce got locked up."

"I know. Legend has to head back to Chicago to see his P.O. The lawyer thinks it's best."

"Well, whatever it is, I just don't want the past to come back haunting us. We all moved here for something better. Chicago is a great city, but those babies are dying every day. Kids are growing up without their fathers and that ain't good. My brother, Troy, and Duce are the men in our lives. We just need to open their eyes and let them know what it is. I don't want to bury no more of our people."

"I hear you."

We sat and talked a little bit more before I saw my niece and left. The moment I walked out to my car, a police car was right next to it. I just shook my head.

"I'm tryna figure out what team you're on. Pretty soon, I will have every last one of them in my hands, especially the Legend," some fat ass cop told me with those yellow ass teeth. I didn't respond or say shit. I hopped in my car and alerted all of them. I've been around this shit long enough to know when the cops are tryna scare people. Not I.

THIRTY-TWO

ONARI

"Hi, Ms. Williams, how are you feeling?" My doctor came with one of the nurses.

"I'm doing better." I was up and moving around as usual. I haven't felt any muscle pain, or in my abdomen, so I know my body was healing well. I just needed to take it easy because I could have a setback.

"Let me take a look at your scar." I laid down on the bed and pulled my shirt up. She pressed down on it a little, and I felt the pain a little, but not like before.

"You're healing very fast. We ran all your test, and today is the day you can go home. Everything is fine. I just want you to keep exercising your body to keep that strength up. As for baby Princess, she will be here until she gains some weight."

I told her ok and felt some type of way. I honestly didn't want to go home. I didn't want to be around Legend or even leave my baby here.

"You ready?" Legend walked in the room.

The tension was still there, and I wasn't fucking with him on any level. I think he thought I was going to sweep this shit under the rug since we've been ok after I had the baby. I'm just tryna stay sane. I didn't even respond. I just took a shower and got dressed. When we got down to the car, he grabbed my arm, and I pulled away.

"How many times do I have to say I'm sorry? I thought everything was good now." He looked like a sad puppy.

"You don't have to. I don't need to hear it," I said, and he opened the door for me. I got inside and just looked out the window. I knew if I wanted to block out everything, I needed to focus on something other than his cheating ass.

Once we got to the house, I could tell that he had been here, but I didn't think he would have everything set up since he was in Chicago for a couple of days. I walked straight to my room and hopped on the computer. The first thing I did was sent in my application to have my daycare opened down here. The only thing I needed to do was go to a couple of classes, and I should be good. I already had my money saved up, so I didn't even have to use the money Legend put in my account. I wanted to give that shit back, but it would be another argument.

"Can we talk?" he came in and sat next to me.

"About?"

"Come on, ma. It's been too many days that we haven't been ourselves. What do I have to do to get you to trust me again? Yes, I fucked up, but I can't let you go like that. This shit is crazy."

I slowly turned around in my chair to face him.

"Legend I don't want to do this. I don't care what goes on in our relationship. I would have never stepped out on you. You were so pissed, instead of coming to ask me who Kane was, you decided to go fuck the next bitch tryna get back at me. Kane was nowhere near as important in my life. You were, but obviously you didn't feel the same way."

"Get the fuck out of here. You are my everything. I was drunk and didn't think. I didn't stick my dick in them. It wasn't even like that. One bitch pulled my pants down, and they both sucked my dick. That was it. I love you and only you."

He grabbed my hands, but I pulled them away.

"So, it's ok if I go out and let a nigga like Kane eat my pussy. It means nothing right. I didn't cheat, right?" He didn't answer, but his facial expression told me to stop talking.

"Fuck all that. I just need you to trust me."

"Trust you? I should have followed my first mind and never let you in my life. Yes, we have history, but I fucked up letting you into my personal world. You sold me all these lies, and now I'm looking stupid. I'm looking stupid while the bitch who sucked your dick is laughing. You niggas don't think until it's too late. I'm good, Legend."

"Stop, ma. Please."

"It hasn't even been a full year and look what's happening. This shit was way too soon." He kept trying to grab my hands.

"I just want to be left alone. I need to focus on my kids, my happiness, and myself, not what you're doing in the streets."

"I can respect that. I'ma give you some time, but I promise you this ain't over. If it takes forever to gain your trust, then I'm willing to wait. Nobody is perfect, and I'm willing to work on it all to get my girl back," he said and kissed my hand. He walked away, and I just closed the door. I needed some peace.

A WEEK LATER, I was getting bits of good news one after another. The doctors gave us heads up that baby Princess will be home before we know it. She has gained weight like they wanted, but more test needs to be run to ensure she's going to be ok. We've both been back and forth with keeping Aniyah and going to see Princess. I also started my classes to open my shop. In the meantime, I've just been spending time with Aniyah and doing my daily runs.

"I think you need to get out and get some air," Legend's mom Brenda told me.

To stay away from him, I've been coming and going. When I

know he's home, I would purposely visit my grandma or his mom. He knew it and always used the excuse that he misses Aniyah.

"Oh, I am. We all planned a night out in these LA streets. I need it," I said, and she smiled.

"Why didn't I get an invite?"

"It's a young thing. You wouldn't like the music." Brenda always tried to act younger.

"You're right. When y'all stepping out?" We were sitting at her table while she fed Aniyah.

"Tomorrow. It's Friday, so you know the clubs are gone be popping. A friend of mine has opened a club here and wants me to stop by. We just need to get some new fresh air. I need to get a makeover too because I haven't been feeling myself lately."

"I told you you're beautiful. You don't have to go all out prove a point." I smiled.

"I know. It's just a woman thing." I sat and talked with her for a couple more hours before we headed home.

It was nine o'clock when I got in the crib, and Legend was watching sports on the TV. When Aniyah saw him, she instantly ran into his arms. I immediately walked up the stairs.

I just wanted to relax my mind, so I poured me a cold glass of wine, and got inside the Jacuzzi. I didn't even notice I was fast asleep until I felt Legend picking me up out the tub.

"Come on, you tired," he said while wrapping a towel around me. Once I got in the bed, I was knocked all the way out and didn't even feel him climb in beside me.

THE NEXT DAY my phone was ringing like crazy. I knew it was Nastasia. We made an appointment to get dolled up, and I was running late.

"I'm up," I said, climbing out the bed still naked. It was going on noon, so I had to hurry up.

"Bitch, you got twenty minutes to get here," she said, hanging up in my face.

"Where are you going?" Legend came behind me with nothing on but his boxers. All I could see was his big ass dick just hanging. He was sweating bullets, and my eyes could only focus on his dick.

"To get my hair done." I quickly grabbed my robe and walked inside the bathroom, and he followed me.

"You got something planned?"

"Not really," I lied. I knew if I told him my plans. He would pop up. Plus I didn't want him knowing that I was going to Kane's club.

"Ok, well hurry up because I fixed you breakfast." I caught him eyeing my ass.

Yes, I had another baby, and now my hips and ass are off the chain. My stomach went back flat like before, and the only thing I needed to work on was getting rid of this scar on my stomach.

"Ok."

Once I finished showering and putting my clothes on, I headed down the stairs. I had a pair of blue jeans, a tank top, and my flat sandals.

"Can I take you out later?" he asked me while sitting my plate in front of me.

"I had plans with the girls. If I get back in time, then yea," I said just so he wouldn't go lurking on my plans.

"Get back in time?" he questioned. I knew he wouldn't stop.

"Check this out. I'ma come pick you up after you finish getting your hair done."

"Ok." I left it alone so that nothing would look suspicious.

Once I finished eating, I ran up the stairs like I forgot something. I already had my bag packed just in case he got on bullshit. I stuffed it in my big ass purse and came back down.

"See you later, mama." I kissed Aniyah and jumped in my car. It was hot as hell, but I needed this air.

WE SAT in the shop for almost five hours before we were done. I had my hair flat ironed then curled all the way down my back.

"Now this is the Onari I knew," Nastasia said, and I began taking pictures of myself.

"I even feel much better." I was grinning hard because I've been feeling off lately.

"Ok, we gotta get going. I need to have a couple of drinks before we head out." I followed Nastasia in my car. Once we got to her crib, Troy was there, and I knew he was going to tell Legend.

"Bitch, we gotta make it quick. I don't want to run into him. I just want to enjoy myself." She already knew the deal.

"Ok, let's hurry and get dressed." While we got dolled up, Tisha and Solo popped up with a bottle of D'usse.

"Don't even ask where's the wine because tonight you're drinking nothing but dark," Solo told my ass, and I didn't argue.

"I'm just tryna figure out who are you seeing tonight?" Tisha said, laughing.

I was wearing some high waisted pants with a half shirt showing a little of my back and stomach. Only Nastasia knew where we were going. I figured if I told Solo, he would go and tell Legend.

"I thought you were insecure about your skin?" Nastasia said, admiring my come back.

"I thought about it all, and I can't change what happened, so now I have to deal with it. If Legend doesn't like it, then oh well. Someone else will." I know my mouth was reckless, but I didn't care.

"Ok. Let's drink." Solo poured us all a cup, and we headed out the door.

"Girl, yo ass is just too big for me. You're gone get in trouble tonight," Tisha said making me blush.

"That's the plan," I said, and our night began.

THIRTY-THREE

LEGEND

"What up, my nigga?"

I looked up and that nigga Duce was out like it wasn't shit. He was too happy for me. I already got the news that they were letting him go and dropped the charges. They didn't have enough evidence and figured she was just hurt behind Pike getting killed. Now Kane is a different story.

"You come in loud. What's the word?" I said, sitting Aniyah on the couch so that she could watch cartoons while I cook breakfast.

"Same shit. I'm out, so now I can get back to my money and my girl."

Tisha said fuck him and was seen with a whole new nigga. It wasn't my business, so I didn't even bring it up. I got my own problems.

"She still pissed?" he sat at the table and asked about Onari.

"Hell, yea. I've been trying everything." I was salty.

"You gotta try harder, son." Duce's granddad walked in. He went to pick Duce up, so they both stopped by.

"I've been trying." I was all out of options.

"Your head is too far in the game. You got a good woman by your side. You don't get that these days. You gotta go after her. Don't take no for an answer from her. You gotta go harder now because she doesn't trust you. Believe me. I cheated on my wife one time, and that's all it took. It took her years to finally trust me again.

While he was talking, I walked to the closet and pulled a small gift bag out. Inside was the ring I had bought to propose to her, but shit just went downhill.

"I can't go no harder than this, right?" I said, sitting the ring on the table.

"You gotta make this one special. It can't be the norm. It's gotta be different. Get yo shit together." His granddad was straight up honest. I knew I had to come hard. We've been having small conversations, but that was it.

"Where is she?" Duce asked while playing with Aniyah.

"I've been letting her get some rest, so I get up early with Aniyah most of the time. I don't want her to feel overwhelmed with worrying about Princess and Aniyah."

"How is Princess doing?" his granddad asked me.

"She will be home soon. I'ma give it another month, and she should be here. She will be almost two months." I was happy. I just wanted my family all together.

"I know the perfect time to bring that ring out," Duce said, and I was skeptical about taking his advice.

"When?"

"Her birthday is coming up. Go hard or go home, right?" This wasn't the Duce I knew. I thought he would say some wild shit like a stripper party or something.

"I'ma set some shit up. I'ma need y'all help though."

"I got you. Just focus on y'all first. You got enough time before her birthday to get ya shit together." I thought long and hard about what his granddad said.

Once they left, I cooked Onari some breakfast and started working on the proposal. My first step was figuring out where her mind was at. I know she wanted to open her shop, so I made sure to go all out and get it started. I already bought a couple of buildings, so now I gotta bring it to life.

———

"YO, you heard from Onari? She went to get her hair done and never came back home. We made plans to go out, and now she's not answering." I called my mom because I knew Onari would stop by there a lot before coming home.

"Naw, she didn't stop here today. Call Nastasia," she said like she wasn't too worried. I knew then she already knew where Onari was. I just hung up and called everybody phone. The only person who answered was Troy.

"Is Onari over there?" I got right to it.

"They went out to the club, bro." I damn near jumped through the phone.

"Say no more. Meet me there," I said and hung up.

I quickly got dressed in all black and woke Aniyah up. I packed her a bag because I got a feeling I'ma be out all night long. Onari had me all the way fucked up. As soon as I dropped Aniyah off to Ms. Rosie, I fled to the club and parked directly behind Onari's car. I hopped out, and Duce and Troy were just pulling up.

We all walked to the door, and the bouncer greeted us and let us in with no problem.

"Don't do shit stupid. Just pull her to the side and take her home," Troy said, but seeing all of them turning up pissed me off. Tisha was giving some nigga a lap dance, and Onari was dancing with some lame ass nigga. He was grabbing her hips, and I lost it.

Duce didn't even wait to confront them. He pulled his gun out and shot in the air, busting the lights. Everyone screamed, including them. When Onari saw my face, she took off running.

"Block the fucking door!" I yelled to the bouncer, but he was too slow.

She flew out the door, and I was on her heels. Once we all got outside, she ran in the opposite direction of her car, so I jumped in my car and chased her down. She was running fast as hell, but not too fast to where I couldn't catch her. When she tried to run into the alley, I drove in behind her, and she was stuck.

"Legend, stop!" she yelled and started screaming like I was going to kill her.

"Man, shut the fuck up before I give you a reason to scream," I said and grabbed her by the arm. I literally drugged her to the car and pinned her against it.

"Why you got me out here acting a fool? Huh? Then you dancing all on that nigga like it wasn't shit. Matter of fact, take me to him." I pulled my gun out my waist, and she freaked out.

"No, Legend. Stop."

"Ain't no stop. I love the fuck outta you, but you not finna play me. Seeing his hands all over your ass doesn't sit well with me." I was all in her face, and she was terrified.

"Kane invited me to his club, so I figured I would go to hurt you. The same way you hurt me," she quickly blurted out, and I had to take a step back. I rubbed my chin trying hard not to pull the trigger.

"That nigga told you that? Are you crazy or stupid? This is my homie big Tone's spot. That nigga Kane doesn't even know shit about Cali. He set yo goofy ass up to get fucked up in these streets." She began looking around like someone was supposed to rescue her.

"Come on, bro. Y'all niggas got me out here running. I'm too fat for this shit," Troy said out of breath.

"Let's go," I said, and she didn't argue. I put her in the car and gave Solo and the rest of them a death stare.

"Onari, you good?" Nastasia said, and I answered.

"She's good," I said and told them to take Onari's car home.

When I got in the car, it was nothing but silence. She was looking out the window, and the tears were coming down her cheeks. I felt fucked up on the inside. I just reached over and wiped them. Shit was never supposed to be like this. All I wanted to do was love her and protect her.

When we pulled in the driveway, it started pouring down, and she got out and slammed the door.

"Onari, stop ma. Hear me out." She had me all the way confused with this love shit.

Listening to what my lawyer told me, I quickly grabbed her arms and pulled her towards me. I just held her, and she looked me in my eyes. For every tear that fell down her face that came from my bullshit, I had to replace it. I had to replace it with my heart.

"Please. Ma. Please. I'm begging you to give me that hope. Give me back all of you. I know you don't trust me right now, but I can promise you I will never hurt you again. I need you to let me back in. I don't want my girls growing up without you and me by each other's side. I just want my family back." We were both getting wet up, but I didn't give a fuck.

"How can I just let you come back so soon? Legend, I'm hurting. I literally dropped everything and followed you. You gave me a dream, and you sold it. You sold it." She slowly pulled away and began walking towards the door.

"Tell me right now that you're willing to walk away from me. Tell me this is it, and I will leave you alone. I will take care of my girls, and that's it." She continued to walk, so I took that as we were done. I was lowkey hurt, but it is what it is. I just opened my car door and was about to climb in.

"The problem is I know I can't live without you. I dreamed of a man like you, Legend. I don't want to start all the way over." I closed the door, and she literally ran into my arms crying like a baby. I picked her up and held her.

"Then let me back in, ma. Let me back in, and I promise I'ma give you and my girls the world. Whatever you need I'ma deliver. I ain't shit without you. You hear me." I grabbed her head and forcefully kissed her lips.

"Yes." I didn't even want to put her down. I just held her because I felt good at that moment. I got my girl back.

"Yessss! Yessss!" Troy and Nastasia were just pulling up. The big ass smile across my face was all they needed to see.

"Now get yo shit together, bro. She's a good one. Marry that lady!" he yelled, and I was going to do just that.

I carried her in the house and tossed her on the couch. I stood, and she watched me strip down to my birthday suit. I ain't had no pussy in almost two months.

"Take that shit off," I demanded, and she did just that. Seeing how big her ass and titties got had my mouth watering. I picked her up and sat her on the counter.

"Mmmm, fuck. Daddy."

I began licking and sucking all over her neck, then made my way down to her pretty pink ass nipples, one of my favorite things to do. I then pulled her to the edge of the counter, opened her legs as wide as they would go, and dove into her pussy. My baby had the best juices ever.

"Ahhhh, fuck! Legend, baby, I love you."

I stuck my tongue all the way inside her pussy, making sure I hit those walls. It didn't take long before I could feel her about to explode. I then pulled out.

"Nooo. Babe," she whined, but I wasn't done.

I picked her up and carried her up to our balcony. This was some shit we've never done before, but I knew she was all for it. Just watching the rain come down, and the beautiful view in front of us was everything. Nothing but palm trees and different types of flowers surrounded our backyard.

"I love you, girl," I said, turning her back towards me. I had her hold onto the rail tight, and I opened her legs as far as they would go. I slowly slid my dick into her wet opening, sending her into a frenzy.

"Shhhiiitttt!" I moaned because the way her pussy gripped my dick gave me chills. I had to take my time because then it would be over.

"I miss this dick so much," she moaned while looking into the sky.

I held her from behind and fucked her into a coma. Any moaning and screaming was blocked out from the rain coming down.

"Don't you ever threaten to leave me. You hear me?"

"Yes, daddy, I'm sorry." I instantly pulled out when I felt my nut build up.

I pulled her inside the room and laid her on the bed. I was ready to make love to her. I climbed on top of her and made love to her body, mind, and soul. Massaging my hands all around her pussy caused cum to ooze out, and she begged me to go all in.

"Please babe. I need to feel you inside of me," I smirked and delivered to the fullest. I put her legs on my shoulders and fucked her insides up. Just watching my dick appear and disappear caused me to talk shit.

"Who dick is this?"

"Mine!" she screamed.

"This dick is all yours. Don't ever forget that."

"I love you." I felt her pussy tighten around my dick, and she again yelled my name.

"Ggggrrr!" I came behind her and exploded. I tried to pull out, but it was useless.

"This shit is forever," I told her and collapsed on top of her.

"Forever it is," she replied and kissed my lips. We fucked all night long until the sun came up. Now, I gotta show my baby the world.

THIRTY-FOUR

DUCE

"On everything I love, Tisha is a dead one."

When I saw her at the party, she dipped on my ass. I don't even know where she went. She wouldn't answer the phone or shit. I then found out that she was with some new nigga like shit was sweet.

"It's been a week and she still ain't fucking with you," Legend said while we were in the mall looking at rings. He had already bought a ring for Onari, but he wanted something bigger.

"Bro, I'm going crazy. Just thinking about another nigga fucking her is about to drive me crazy." She basically said fuck me.

"You can't blame nobody but yourself. That girl went above and beyond for you. She left her family in Chicago thinking this move to Cali was for y'all." Legend picked up a ring that cost damn near two million dollars.

"Bitch, you a sucka. You all in love in shit now. You better get her ass a Walmart ring." He laughed, but I was for real. If I buy a ring for that much, we had better be together for two million lifetimes.

"When you find that one, you'll get this same feeling. I fucked up, but I'm a man of my word. I love that girl and I'ma give it a couple of months, and we gone be married. I can't live without her. Call me what you want, but I'm happy," Legend said, trying to make me soft like him.

"I'm still beating her ass."

"You got hard feelings for Tisha. You just scared to show it. Man up, bro. You ain't getting no younger. Don't wait too late then she falls in love with another nigga."

I didn't even respond. I knew he was right. While I was in jail those couple of days, those bitches I was chasing never checked on me. They didn't even answer the phone for a nigga. I knew if Tisha weren't pissed, she would have come with no problem.

"We gotta do better. I fucked up and almost lost my girl. You fucked up, but now you gotta get your girl back," Legend said, and when we finished, he stopped at a couple of stores to get some things.

"What the fuck are you doing in Victoria Secret?" I asked before walking in the store. This nigga was bugging now.

"I'ma surprise Onari with some sexy lingerie. She likes that type of stuff. You need to be shopping as well," Legend said and was so sure of himself. He wasn't ashamed either. I just shook my head and laughed. My boy done changed on a nigga.

"We need some help!" he yelled, and I tried to act like I wasn't with him.

"My boy is looking for some sexy shit," he blurted out, and the girl laughed.

"What he means is that my girl is looking for some sexy shit," I tried to reverse that shit.

"So, your girl sent you here to find her some lingerie?"

"Yea, now what you got?" I said bout ready to knock Legend out. He used me so he wouldn't walk in asking for the lingerie.

"On everything, I got you, nigga. You foul for this."

"Nigga, just get the shit and let's roll."

We both shopped until we couldn't carry shit else. I even bought Tisha some red bottoms and some jewelry. I wasn't on the level with Legend, but I gotta start somewhere.

We were out all day, and then when his phone started blowing up, we headed home. I was hungry as hell, so when I got back to my crib, I whipped me up some burgers and fries. As soon as I sat down to eat, I heard some noise. I jumped up and grabbed my gun, ready to blast whoever. Once I made it to the door, I pulled it out and aimed.

"Ahhhhh! It's me." Tisha was standing there, and when I looked down, piss was running down her legs.

"I know the fuck you didn't piss on my doorstep." I put the gun down.

"I need to pee really bad, and your house was close. Then you made it worse by trying to kill me." I pulled her inside and shut the door.

"Take yo pissy ass upstairs and washed that shit off. When you finish, come down so that you can eat," I demanded, and she did.

Tisha and I had this weird ass relationship. When we love, we love hard. When we hate, we go all the way. When I found out she was getting too close to another nigga, I was ready to tear some shit up. Then she had the nerve to be giving some nigga a lap dance like it was cool.

When she came down, I sat her plate in front of her, and she tried to avoid eye contact. She had on one of my t-shirts and boxer shorts.

"You're really gone sit here and act like what you did wasn't wrong?"

"What did I do, Donte? You turned your back on me as soon as we got up here. All I wanted was for us to grow up and grow together. All that street shit is not cool. Then you just out fucking bitches like I don't mean shit to you. I don't care what our relationship status was. I would have never embarrassed you like that. Bitches are sitting back laughing, and you don't see that."

"Man, fuck them hoes. It's always been you and me. Yea, I've been doing a lot lately, but they don't mean shit to me. You do." I could see she was hurting.

"And the dude I was with don't mean shit to me." She was tryna to get under my skin, and it was working.

"You think I won't peel that nigga head right in front of you?"

"Donte, shut up. If you really wanna know, he is working with me to take Kane down. When you got locked up, I did some digging, and Kane was basically out to get y'all because of his brother being killed. When that shit happened with Pike and Rondo, he pulled in Pike's baby momma to help. The problem is they had no evidence. They figured that if they came to Cali, they could get close to someone, someone like Onari. I don't think she knows anything, but they're trying to ruin y'all," she laid it out, and I wasn't surprised.

"They can't ruin shit. That's why I got out. They don't have no evidence," I said while grabbing my phone.

I sent the emergency text to Legend and Troy to meet me later. I was finna dead this shit once and for all. The fact that he lied to Onari and told her he had a club let me know that this nigga Kane was on some other shit.

"Just don't do nothing stupid. You moved all the way out here for a better life. Whether you and I are on to something else, I don't want you going down." I frowned and stood up.

"It's gone always be you and me. Fuck all them hoes. I just want you," I said, and she knew I was serious.

"We have a lot to work on. I don't want to rush everything knowing how you are. I don't want to hear it. I need to see it."

"I got you. Just don't make me bury yo ass for playing with me." She smirked, and I got up to give her the gifts I bought. When she opened the box of shoes, she frowned.

"Donte, these are a size nine. I wear a size six. These are some big ass boats."

"Man, yo ass better stuff some tissue in them bitches. Those shoes cost damn near seven hundred dollars." She was laughing, but I was serious.

"Open the other bag," I told her. When she pulled out the lingerie, she laughed.

"Who is this for, Donte? I am a big boned female. I have an ass out of this world. Does it look like I wear a size ¾? I can't fit this."

I told Legend she wouldn't be able to fit this shit. Now I gotta take everything back.

"It's cool. At least you tried. We gone work on that and work on us. Apparently, we don't know a lot about each other." I picked up a fry and threw it at her. I ain't gone lie. It felt real good to have Tisha back.

"I didn't forget you shot me in my ass either. I'ma get you back one day." My ass had finally healed, but I got a big ass scar that will be permanent.

"You gone be ok," she said and began eating her food.

We laid around and talked all day until the wee hours of the morning. The crazy part was that I was enjoying every bit of her. I would normally want to fuck, but that wasn't even on my mind. Her company was enough.

AFTER MEETING with Troy and Legend, we decided it was time to put a stop to this shit. What was so crazy was that we didn't even have to look for Kane. He spotted us and tried to make a scene. We were inside a seafood restaurant just talking shit.

"Y'all niggas are real fuckin' grimy. Y'all gone kill my brother then gone act like it wasn't y'all."

I could tell he was high off something because his eyes were twitching, and his breath smelt like shit.

"Bruh, what's that smell? Is that dookie?" Troy told him, and everyone in the restaurant started laughing. He didn't like that shit.

"Naw, I'ma smoke yo ass." he pointed the gun at Troy, and everyone ran.

We were calm because he wasn't too crazy. A real nigga would have shot without even talking. Legend was calm, but I already knew shit was finna get real for his ass.

"I'ma give y'all a pass for right now, but I'ma see y'all again," he said and walked off like a crackhead.

"That you will," Legend replied under his breath.

"Let's roll before the police come."

We all got up and left. We began looking around and apparently his ass was gone and nowhere in sight. That's a crackhead for you.

"He's bringing too much heat. This shit doesn't look good," Legend said, and I agreed. After tonight, everything would be over.

THIRTY-FIVE

ONARI

As bad as I wanted to walk away from Legend, I just couldn't. That man had me stuck. Yes, he fucked up, but we all do. As of right now, we're focused on our little family. I realized I could have lost it all being blind to Kane's bullshit. That fucked me up when they told me he didn't have a club and didn't even live in Cali. I still didn't understand why he chose me. I wasn't even with Legend when his brother was killed.

"Hey, mommy's Princess. Look at you." I was sitting Indian style on the bed, just in awe of my Princess. When we got the news that she could come home, I was beyond happy. Legend made sure that we had everything we needed.

"Dada." Aniyah ran to the stairway when she heard him come in the house.

"Hey, daddy baby." He came up and picked her up. He came over, kissed me, and rubbed my face. I could see he had a worried look.

"Talk to me," I said and handed him the baby.

"When I moved down here, I tried to leave all the bullshit back in

Chicago. Naw man, that nigga Kane and Pike's baby momma are on bullshit," he said too calm for me.

"Pike's baby momma?" I said, surprised. I didn't know where this was going, or if he was going to spazz, so I stood up.

"Back then we had dealings with Kane's brother, which you already know, he snitched on everyone and later he was found dead. Before you ask, no, I didn't kill him. Knowing that he was all in your face to get at me got me ready to bug the fuck up, but then I keep telling myself if I do something stupid, I'ma go back down. Niggas are testing my gangsta because I'm not who I used to be." That look in his eye told me he was about to do something stupid. I just picked Princess up and laid her in the baby bed.

"I'm sorry for allowing him to even get close and have a conversation. I didn't know, and now I regret it," I said, and he pulled me down onto his lap. He didn't say anything. He just grabbed the back of my head and kissed my lips.

"Don't ever apologize for something you knew nothing about. I try to keep you out the loop because of shit like this. Now, I'm pissed because I didn't tell you. Then the nigga just popped up on us with a gun. He was high off some shit and was buggin'.'"

I just rubbed his face and head.

"I just want you to focus on what's in front of us. You or anyone of y'all reacting will not look good. You got good news when your parole officer decided to transfer your papers down here. That's a sign, babe. I can't do this without you. You hear me."

"I hear you, ma. I love the fuck out of you." He kissed me until Aniyah began cock blocking.

"Dada. Dada." She was pulling at his shirt, and we laughed.

"Daddy is showing too much attention to her. I'm sorry, ma."

"She's gotta go back to Brenda's. She's doing too much now."

"Mommy's a hater." Aniyah was now happy. He walked with her downstairs while I hopped in the shower.

It was hot as fuck outside, so I had to keep the air on low so that Princess wouldn't get sick.

HOURS LATER, I was chilling in my bed, feeding Princess, and watching this new show on Netflix called *All American*.

"She finally went to sleep, babe. I'm tired now." It was just getting dark, and Legend was beat. He laid across the bed and kissed Princess' forehead.

"How you been feeling?" he asked me. One thing Legend always does is check and make sure that I'm ok. That's how much he cares.

"I'm ok. I feel whole again," I said, smiling.

"That's all I'm tryna do." We talked a little bit more before Princess was knocked out cold.

"Come here," he told me while pulling my shirt over my head. He then laid on the bed, and I climbed on top of him. The same way that my man pleases me, I do the same for him. I licked and sucked on him until he was damn near empty. The way he had my hair wrapped around his hands let me know I was the shit.

"Turn around. I need to see that ass jiggle."

I did as he said, and he pounded my insides out. He fucked me so good that I damn near cried when my juices started flowing. We fucked until two in the morning, and then after that, I couldn't move. I literally slept like a baby on his chest.

HOURS LATER, I looked up, and the clock read seven a.m.

"Babe," I called his name. He didn't answer, so I got up to check on the kids.

I figured he was downstairs with them. Once I got halfway down, the silence made me stop. Every morning my house is lit because of Aniyah. She has to watch her cartoons every morning. My instincts kicked in, and I knew something was wrong. I decided to stay quiet, and when I got down the stairs, I noticed the front and side door was still locked. I picked up the phone we got in the kitchen and dialed

Duce and Troy. This phone was only for emergencies, so when the number pop up, they will know to get here asap.

I quickly threw my shoes on and grabbed the Glock he had right by the basement door. I tried to stay calm because right now, I wasn't sure what was going on. I wasn't good at shooting yet, but as of right now, I was ready for whatever. I tried not to think of my babies being hurt, but I know Legend wouldn't allow that. I tried to think positive, and not to be scared. I slowly opened the door, and to my surprise, it didn't creak or make a sound.

"I should blow ya head off. Onari is supposed to be mine."

I slowly walked down the stairs, and I spotted Kane and Pike's baby momma with guns drawn on Legend. I didn't see the babies, but the look Legend was giving me let me know to be cool. No words were needed. I continued walking down the stairs, and with their backs turned against me, I slowly crept up on them.

"Where yo bitch now? Her little burnt body ass is probably fuckin' the next nigga she comes in contact with." The blow was definitely a low one, but I shrugged it off.

"Naw, my burnt body ass is right here." They quickly turned around and tried to react, but it was too late. Legend pulled both guns from his waist and shot both of them.

"Ahhh, fuck!" Kane yelled once the bullet entered his back. He instantly killed Pike's baby momma with one shot to the back of the head. That was straight suicide. I should have felt bad knowing she was pregnant, but obviously, she didn't care.

"That a girl." Legend walked up to me, grabbed the gun out my hand, and told me to get the babies. He had them inside one of the rooms upstairs.

I should have known he was already on it. I quickly ran up the stairs and bumped into Troy, and Duce. They were loaded, so I made sure to close the room door because shit was about to get real.

POW! POW! was all I heard.

The kids were still sleeping, and I could breathe now. Knowing my kids were in danger made me sick to my stomach.

THIRTY-SIX

LEGEND

I couldn't stop thinking about this bum ass nigga Kane. The fact that he thought it was ok to pull a gun on us and repercussions weren't gone apply was crazy. Then he did it in front of everyone, and that pissed me off. I had to play this shit cool because I didn't want to alarm Onari. Her trust was already on thin ice when it comes to me, so I decided to tell her. Hearing those words and her telling me to basically think about our family, made me chill out.

Once I put Onari to sleep, I couldn't help but think. My mind was going crazy, and I felt something in the pit of my stomach. Not thinking twice, I got up and grabbed my guns. As soon as I looked up at one of the cameras, I spotted two dummies trying to get in the basement door. The crazy part was I knew it was Kane. This nigga had the balls to follow me home. He was bold. I didn't want to wake Onari because I didn't know how she would react. I grabbed the babies since they were still sleeping and put them in the guest bedroom. I laid Princess down gently in the baby bed and laid Aniyah on the bed.

I quietly shut the door and put the code in. I alerted the guys and went down the stairs. I checked the cameras again, and I didn't see them. I knew they got inside. Before going down, I put my bullet-proof vest on and slowly opened the door. As soon as I got down the stairs, I caught the nigga tryna take my speakers.

"Look who's here," Kane said with some white shit all over his face. I knew he wasn't all there. He was on another planet.

"Drop it and stand over here," he said, and I did.

I dropped my gun and tried to keep my eye on his gun. I don't even think he had bullets in it. This nigga was beyond crazy. They had me get in the corner, and my plan was working. One thing about me was that I always thought ahead. I had two guns inside my pants. The one I was told to drop was all a part of the plan.

"Fuck you think you doing?" He had the girl to grab anything of value. I just shook my head.

"Shut the fuck up, bitch. You a hoe ass nigga."

I kept it cool, and as soon as I spotted Onari coming down with the gun, I knew it was over for them. The bitch got to talking crazy, so when Onari made her presence be known, I took over. They each turned to look at her, and I pulled both my guns out that I had hidden and fired.

I blew her head to pieces and shot him in the back.

"That a girl," I told Onari, and I took the gun out her hand. I told her where the girls were, and she went back upstairs — no words needed to be said.

"What the fuck?" His bitch ass was on the floor in a lot of pain. I knew he would die soon because I hit his ass with a hollow tip. I was about to end it, but when Troy and Duce came down ready for war, it was over. Duce raised his gun and shot him twice in the chest. He was no longer moving.

"Call the lawyer and the police. They done broke in my crib," I said, and Troy laughed.

I was dead serious. I didn't need anything coming back on me, so I reported the break-in and made sure my cameras caught every angle of them breaking in. My guns weren't registered because I am a convicted felon, but I know my Lawyer gone handle that situation.

All I got to do is show proof of me doing everything the legal way, and how the street shit is over with.

"You're smart, bro," Duce said, and we didn't touch shit.

I made Onari stay upstairs with Duce and Troy until I was finished with everything. I didn't even want them to know they were here. Shit would go downhill from there.

About thirty minutes later, cops surrounded my home, and I turned the guns in and gave then the surveillance footage. I let them investigate, while me and my lawyer waited on what they had to say.

"You know I got this in the bag. That cop is a longtime friend of mines. Your good." He said and I smiled. I knew he would come through.

"After doing some digging, we didn't find any connections between you or them. This was the second robbery in this neighborhood, and we think they were behind that one as well. Right now, it looks like a robbery gone wrong, so I'm going to have you and your lawyer meet me at the station to clear some things up."

I kept it cool and told him ok. When he left, I gave Troy and Duce the heads up to stay there until I come back. I will deal with cleaning that shit up later.

I SPENT hours at the station before I was released. When I got back to the crib, everyone was there, including Ms. Rosie. She was pissed.

"Please tell me they dropped the charges?"

"Yes. It's all over now," I said, knowing that he was dead and gone. I didn't have to worry about them going to the police and trying to bring us down.

"Thank god. My grandbabies could have gotten hurt."

"I was gone die for mine. Onari handled it very well," I said, winking at her.

I needed a strong drink after this, and that's what I did. I got so damn drunk that the last thing I remembered was the ladies playing cards, and me and the guys talking more money moves.

ONE MONTH Later

"Bro you did ya motherfuckin' thang. She's gone love this." After spending countless, sleepless nights, I finally found the perfect spot for Onari to open her daycare here in Cali. I called in a lot of help, and we finished everything inside in under four days.

"Thanks, sis. Now how long is she gone be before she gets here?" I was so thirsty because today is the day I'ma ask her to marry me. It's also her birthday. I made this shit look real. The decorator did her thang as well with the cakes and liquor fountains. My baby deserves it all.

"She just finished getting her hair done, and now she's at home getting dressed." Onari thinks she's going out to eat with the ladies, but it's all a setup.

"I'm proud of you, bro. You're finally about to lock her down." Troy gave me a brotherly hug.

"Nigga, you looking real sharp today too. I see the Fendi loafers. Straight boss shit." I laughed, and we shook up.

"I gotta make her, Mrs. Jackson. She deserves the world," I was smiling hard as hell.

"That's my son-in-law. I love you, kid," Ms. Rosie said. I hugged her and whispered in her ear.

"Thank you for trusting me with her. I promise you that it's all up from this point."

"I know. I know, son." Everyone was showing me love, and when I got the news that she was five minutes away, I told everyone to hide.

As soon as she got out of the car and parked, we could hear her loud ass mouth.

"Solo, this don't look like no damn restaurant. Y'all are on some bullshit. Legend is gone kill me if he finds out I'm lying."

"Shut up, girl," he told her, and when the door opened, we all screamed surprise and Happy birthday.

She literally turned and was about to run, but Solo grabbed her. We all laughed.

"Surprise ma, it's your very own daycare." Her mouth was wide open, and she was speechless.

"Say something, girl," my mom said, and Onari began crying.

"Thank you so much, babe. You did this for me?" She walked up to me and hugged me.

"Most definitely. Whatever you want, I'ma always deliver," I said, and she kissed my lips.

"Come open the gift he got you," Ms. Rosie told her knowing what my next move was. While she stood at the table opening my gifts, I got behind her on one knee and pulled the ring out. I was shaking like a leaf, but I didn't fold.

"Onari, you know you're my world, right?" I said, and she slowly turned around. Her seeing me on one knee made her bawl.

"OMG!" She made everyone else cry, and a nigga almost folded.

"I love you to the moon and back. I know I fucked up when I brought you into this crazy ass life of mine, but you held me down. We got a year into this relationship, but that's not enough. I'm looking for a lifetime. I'm looking for forever. There is no me without you. All I ask is you make me the happiest man on earth and let me give you my last name. Onari Shanel Williams, will you marry me?" She jumped up and down just screaming.

"Yes, babe! Yes. I would love to be Mrs. Jackson." She jumped in my arms, and I placed the ring on her finger.

"That's what the fuck I'm talking about. That's my nigga!" Duce yelled already drunk. Since he was back with Tisha, he had changed just a little. They argued like cats and dogs, but I knew the love they had for each other overpowered anything on the outside.

"Thanks, bro."

Now that the news was out, it was party time. We all got drunk as fuck, and before the clock struck twelve, I took my baby to a small resort and the night was ours.

THIRTY-SEVEN

ONARI

ONE YEAR LATER

"Bitch, stop crying," Tisha said while handing me some napkins. I was currently getting my makeup done. I was all set and ready to walk down the aisle.

"I can't."

"It's gone be ok." We all were dolled up for my big day. I still couldn't believe I was about to get married.

"You've been through a lot, boo. You deserve to be happy from this point forward. Your brothers and parents would be proud of you," Nastasia said, and I smiled. I lost a lot behind everything that went on in Chicago. I literally thought my life was over. I wanted to give up, but the man in Legend wouldn't let me do that. He held me down like he said he would.

"I hope you don't get sick before we get started," Solo said, and I rubbed my growing belly. That's right. A couple of months after I had Princess, I found out I was pregnant once again. Neither of us was in shock because we never used protection. I finally got my boy, and of course, he will be a Jr.

"I hope I don't either." I didn't have as many problems as I did when I was pregnant with Princess, and I was happy as hell.

"Mama." Princess was so spoiled thanks to Legend. He had these girls wrapped around his finger, and now we can't do shit without them.

I gave Princess her bottle, and she wobbled away. As soon as she turned one, she started walking and was fat as hell now. She was bigger than Aniyah, and Aniyah was about to be three.

"Ok. Come on, baby girl. Mommy's got a big day ahead of her." Brenda picked her up, and I got myself together.

After two hours of her doing our makeup, we were all ready. I slowly stood up in my all-white dress and smiled.

"I promise I won't cry."

"Whatever," Tisha said, and everyone laughed. Once they were told that we were ready, I got nervous. Everything popped in my head.

"You're gone be fine," Solo said then walked out.

"You ready?" I looked up and smiled.

Walking me down the aisle was Duce's granddad, Willie. At first, it was hard for me to understand why Legend chose him, but now I understand. I no longer had that male figure in my life, but whenever I was around him, he gave me my daddy vibes. He was so much my father, and that pulled me right in. He became someone I could talk to when times became rough. I know my father was looking down on me with the biggest smile ever.

"Let's roll." Once the music began playing, I let Kem song "Promise to Love" flow through my mind.

"Woman I care for you, and I promise to love. Can we go all the way? You bring me peace to my world, I would anything. You're my love, you are my girl. I, I can see, what your heart has been asking. Do you believe this is love everlasting? Then darlin' I'll marry you, and I promise to love."

Seeing him mouth these words to me let me know how real everything was. Our tears matched, but we held it down. My heart was pounding, but when I made it to him, all of my worries went out the window.

Once the preacher got to talking, I think we both tuned him out. We were both in shock. We didn't even write a speech. When it was time to tell the world why we were made for each other, it just came from the heart.

"At a very young age, I knew you were mine from the moment I first saw you. You were very special to me, and I would always let the world know that you would be mine one day. The day I got out of jail, I had to prove it. I had to prove that I could make you happy for a change. You let me in, and of course, I failed, not once but multiple times. You could have walked away, but you didn't. That let me know how real this really was. What we had was rare, and what we got now is rare. From this day forward, I want to bring you nothing but happiness. I promise to love you forever," Legend said, and everyone clapped and cheered us.

"It took a lot for me to let you into my world. So much so that I kept telling myself he is no good. I kept telling myself to run far away. I look back on it and ask myself what if I did run away? What if I never gave you a chance? We wouldn't be here today?" I cried like a baby.

"My love for you is deeper than the ocean. I don't feel whole without you, Legend. I don't care what we went through. What matters most is that we came and conquered. Our love has just begun, and now I'm ready for forever. I promise to love you, Legend," I said, and he didn't even wait for the preacher to signal us to kiss. All the cheers and claps let me know shit was official. I was now Mrs. Onari Jackson.

Everyone stood to watch us walk out and into the receptionist hall. We got so many hugs, and congratulations, but all I wanted to do was eat and sit. My feet were sore.

"Come give me my first dance," Legend said and grabbed my hands. We both walked to the middle of the floor, and the lights were dimmed. Once the music began to play, I smiled.

"This is my song," I told him while we were wrapped in each other's arms. It was "Everlasting Love" by Tony Terry.

"I know." Legend sang every word to me, and I was just blushing. I couldn't have asked for a better husband.

As I sit back and look on everything that has happened, I thank God. I thank God because I wouldn't be here right now. I would probably be in a fucked up situation or probably even dead. I was shown a different life thanks to Legend. He gave me hope after my accident, and I'm still receiving it. He held me down when I lost both my brothers and never left my side.

The funny thing is I looked at the old Legend when he first got out. I looked at the hood in Legend. His name was powerful in any situation. His name spoke volumes. His name took him to the top. If someone ever asked me what made me choose him, I wouldn't even think twice to answer. I was enticed by a hood legend.

A family is all I ever wanted, and I got just that, my two girls, and now my boy. We're complete as of right now.

"Everlasting love, right?" he whispered in my ear.

"Everlasting love," I repeated, and that was our story.

CPSIA information can be obtained
at www.ICGtesting.com
Printed in the USA
LVHW051514270619
622553LV00002B/333/P

9 781070 128795